HER BILLIONAIRE SECRET ADMIRER

BLACK TIE BILLIONAIRES, BOOK #3

JO GRAFFORD

ISBN: 978-1-944794-53-8

GET A FREE BOOK!

Join my mailing list to be the first to know about new releases, free books, special discount prices, Bonus Content, and giveaways.

https://BookHip.com/JNNHTK

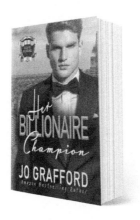

ACKNOWLEDGMENTS

A huge thank you to my editor, Cathleen Weaver! Plus another enormous thank you goes to my beta readers — J. Sherlock, Auntie Em, and Mahasani. I also want to give a shout out to my Cuppa Jo Readers on Facebook. Thank you for reading and loving my books!

CHAPTER 1: KEEPING VIGIL

RHYS

Most men would give anything to walk a day in Rhys Calcagni's shoes. As the Chief Operating Officer of Genesis & Sons, he had billions in investments, a mansion overlooking the gulf, and a last name that opened doors. In the past year alone, it had secured invitations to royal events in no less than seven countries. A five-star chef prepared his meals, an executive assistant managed his jam-packed calendar, and a highly trained security detail guaranteed his safety around the clock.

He literally had it all, minus the one thing he wanted most. Or someone, in his case.

Alora Maddox.

She was never far from his thoughts — the red-gold-haired shining star of his firm's biggest competitor, DRAW Corporation. She was their newly minted CEO, a woman he'd been crushing on since his freshman year of high school. Most unfortunately, she was also his sworn enemy, thanks to a decades-old family feud.

It had been a full twenty-four hours since his last visit with her at the hospital. He couldn't wait to lay eyes on her again and see for himself that she was still pulsing with life beneath all those tubes and wires.

Maybe today will be the day she finally wakes up. He had so much to tell her, things he should have shared with her years ago when he had the chance. Things he'd been too bashful to admit — or cowardly — and now he might never get to.

Her medically-induced coma was approaching three weeks. According to her team of doctors, it was her only hope of surviving the hit-and-run accident that left her silver Lamborghini in a pile of twisted metal. She'd suffered massive amounts of internal damage — a broken neck and shoulder, several fractured ribs, a punctured lung, a ruptured spleen, and an alarming amount of internal bleeding.

While Alora still breathed, however, Rhys refused to give up hope. He was doing everything in his extensive power to ensure her safety while she healed. Over his dead body would the rat-faced scoundrel, who'd attempted to take her life, return to finish the job — not on his watch. He'd cleared his schedule down to the bare bones, so he could personally watch dog over her. Since he worked mostly behind the scenes as Genesis & Sons' key strategist, his time away from the office would not be noted by many.

He stared in agonized contemplation out the tinted, bullet-proof window of his black and silver Bugatti as his chauffeur, Major, carefully steered it up the winding lane to the Gjoa Haven Medical Center. The impeccably landscaped medians on either side of the road were afire with red peonies and orange nasturtium. Cherry laurel lined the front of the building, and stone benches were scattered around the courtyard, providing a place for anxious family members to lounge in the morning sunshine instead of the fluorescent-lit waiting rooms within.

Alora Maddox had no family members visiting her at the intensive care unit today. In some ways, Rhys was to blame for their absence, though it had never been his intention to deprive her of family visits. They were merely under the mistaken impression that she was being guarded around the clock by an elaborately crafted stop-loss measure of her own making before her accident. He'd been careful to ensure that Rand Enterprises, the security firm he'd hired to keep eyes and ears on her 24/7, could not be traced back to him.

Thinking Alora was spinning her usual magic by looking after herself even while fully intubated, her parents had literally left the country — on business, of course, though Rhys considered the distance they'd traveled from her in her current state to be a callous move. Her oldest brother, Greyson, was juggling back-to-back client meetings across town on her behalf; so at least he had a better reason for his absence. Her next younger sister, Bailey, was struggling to absorb the enormous responsibility of running the marketing firm her new husband had recently purchased for her — Titan Industries. Since Titan held an exclusive contract to run all things marketing for DRAW Corporation, Rhys considered Bailey's work to be in direct support of her unconscious sibling.

Her youngest sister, Jacey, was in a category of her own. A pop singing sensation, she'd flown to Nashville last night to record a new single this morning. He had no doubt it would go platinum like the rest of her songs, though he had no idea how she could concentrate enough to sing while her oldest sister's life was hanging in the balance. Of all the Maddox siblings, Jacey and Alora were the closest. Jacey had tearfully called him on his drive to the hospital, begging him to keep her informed of any changes in Alora's condition. She swore she would be back in town before nightfall, thanks to a husband with a pilot's license and a private jet.

Which left only the youngest Maddox brother unaccounted for. According to the feelers Rhys had put out, Kellan Maddox had simply dropped off everyone's radar in the past twenty-four hours. It was puzzling but not necessarily a bad thing, considering Kellan had most likely caused — or at least paid for — the collision that put Alora in the hospital.

When she awoke, it was Rhys's greatest hope she would be capable of pointing a finger at her attacker, so an arrest could be made. Until she awoke, however, there were very few people in the world who knew her car accident wasn't really an accident, and those that loved her wanted to keep it that way.

Rhys was lucky that Alora's inner circle had chosen to include him in that confidence. They probably wouldn't have if they understood exactly how much she despised him. He fully planned to skate across their lack of clarity on the topic for as long as possible. Not to mention, no one in her family would have approved his involvement in her security because of his last name, alone. He and his siblings had been raised to never trust a Maddox; likewise, they'd been raised never to trust a Calcagni.

Major brought the Bugatti to a smooth halt beneath the portico leading to the front glass doors of the hospital.

"Don't get out," Rhys commanded quietly as he opened the passenger door. He had nothing to prove today, no image to maintain in front of the paparazzi. Therefore, there was no reason for his driver to trot around to the passenger door to posture and fawn. Rhys had been very careful to keep this part of his schedule confidential. Besides Major, no one but his executive assistant and newly acquired team of body-guards knew where he was. "Pick me up at a quarter 'til noon at the East entrance."

"Yes, sir." His driver gave him a two-fingered salute.

Rhys grabbed the handle of his Berluti leather briefcase and stepped from the vehicle. Before he could take more than a few steps, Titus Rand silently joined him on the sidewalk. He was a towering hulk of a man with blue-black hair and an exhaustive supply of dark suits and white shirts. He was also a man of few words, which was fine with Rhys. He didn't require a chatty head of security.

Titus's firm, Rand Enterprises, would be exclu-sively serving Rhys for the foreseeable future. Rhys had carefully negotiated their contract a few weeks earlier to ensure he had enough boots on the ground to keep Alora safe at all times. He was exercising every precaution imaginable while guarding the woman he loved, especially since she happened to hold the position of CEO at his firm's top competitor. Too many vultures were circling over the hospital where she lay. One vulture, in particular, had proven he would stop at nothing to steal her title. It was a crying shame that vulture happened to be her own brother.

Rhys and Titus walked in silence through the rotating glass doors of the front entrance and headed for the elevators. Titus had ridden to the hospital on his motorcycle, his preferred mode of transportation. No doubt his Harley was chained like an unruly beast in some shadowy corner of the parking garage.

The elevator light flashed its arrival, and its silver doors rolled open.

"Status update," Rhys demanded softly, after the doors rolled closed behind them.

"I have eyes in the sky and on the ground, sir, as requested."

Rhys nodded. It meant Rand Enterprises had the air space above the hospital guarded as well as a patrol on the perimeter of the facility. "Any news on Kellan?" It was the longest span of time Kellan Maddox had been absent from his oldest sister's bedside the entire time she'd been hospitalized. Those loyal to her had been vigilant, ensuring he had not spent a single moment alone with her.

"None, sir. According to a guy I have on the inside, the last time we had a facial recognition match on the security cams was Tuesday."

It was Thursday morning. Rhys nodded at the women crowded in the nursing station just outside the elevator. They smiled and fluttered their eyelashes at the two men.

"Morning, Mr. Calcagni," the tall, blonde one cooed. Her pupils dilated with appreciation as her gaze swept from him and settled on Titus Rand.

Rhys suppressed a grin. A lesser trained eye than his might have missed Titus's almost imperceptible wince, but Rhys was highly proficient at reading body language. It was a useful skill in and out of the boardroom, one he'd worked diligently to perfect.

He bent his head closer to Titus, speaking in a low tone as they paused outside Alora's bay. "Before you ask, it's too soon to ask for a raise."

Titus's lips twitched. "Figured that, sir."

"Meaning I'd like to go in alone." Leaving Titus outside the bay to bear the lavish admiration of the nursing staff.

"I'll survive, sir." Titus claimed to be ex-military, but Rhys suspected it was something more along the lines of black ops. He didn't particularly care how many secrets the man harbored, so long as he continued to keep Alora alive.

"Thank you." It amused Rhys to no end that Titus sounded like he'd rather be back in the field, dodging bullets and heaven-only-knew what else, as opposed to facing down a fawning nursing staff. However, he genuinely appreciated Titus's willingness to do whatever he was asked. He needed a man of Titus's caliber to have his back right now.

Titus's expression went blank as he assumed a parade-rest stance outside Alora's intensive care bay. Her curtains were drawn. Beyond them, Rhys could hear the whoosh of oxygen and the faint clicking and beeping of machines.

Steeling his heart against the inevitable pain that would accompany what he would see on the other side, he pushed past the curtains and faced Alora Maddox. The curtains closed behind him with a whisper of fabric sliding back into place.

His gaze was drawn first to her luxurious mane of hair, which spilled like fire across her stark white pillow. Her heart-shaped face was an unearthly shade of pale behind the oxygen mask and feeding tube. She looked the opposite of every word he'd seen or heard used to describe her in the tabloids. She was no longer the silver-tongued negotiator or tigress contract writer. She looked delicate and vulnerable beneath her too-still white blankets, like the lightest breeze might sweep her straight off the bed and carry her away from him.

Rhys strode silently to her side, reaching for her hand. "I need you to wake up," he whispered, gently squeezing her slender fingers. They felt cool. He massaged them between both his hands to warm them, noticing how her coral shade of nail polish was farther away from her cuticles than it had been during his last visit. She needed a fresh manicure. He'd notify his executive assistant to send someone before the end of the day to make it happen.

"I need you to wake up, so I can make a proper fool of myself." He settled on the silver stool between her bed and the machine monitoring her vitals. He leaned forward, still cradling her hand between his. "I'm ready to share what's on my heart, so you can reject me once and for all." He bowed his head, lacing his fingers through hers. "I never gave you the chance to do that, did I?"

Instead, he'd hidden his true feelings behind pride and silence — mostly pride. Back during their high school years, he'd been a nerdy guy in glasses and braces. A guy who never failed to make the honor roll. He'd been the president of the math club and chess club. He'd achieved a perfect score on the SAT, and he'd graduated first in his class.

In contrast, Alora swept the popularity votes at her boarding school and served as class president all four years. Somehow, she'd also found the time to preside over their debate team and win their beauty pageant. She was everything he was not — charismatic and vibrant, the darling of the paparazzi.

The fact that she, of all people, had been completely and utterly sidelined by a car accident was a crime against humanity. "I care for you," he vowed softly. "I've felt this way about you for as long as I can remember." Maybe even before high school. "I can't even give you a reason why. I just do." He raised her cool fingers to his mouth to brush his lips against them. "Without you shining your light in the world, I feel like part of me is missing. A part I'll never get back if you don't wake up."

He closed his eyes, his heart aching at the very real possibility that Alora might not ever wake up.

We're doing everything we can. The latest

doctor's report, that Greyson had been kind enough to pass on, echoed dismally through Rhys's head.

It's not enough. Try harder! The ache in his chest settled deeper as he tightened his fingers on Alora's. "Come back to me." He raised her hand to his mouth once more, kissing her delicate fingertips one by one. What he wouldn't give to coax a response from her — any response, no matter how small! It was terrifying and depressing to realize that none of his billions could buy something so precious. Like every other poor Joe, he was stuck firmly in the realm of blind hope — waiting, praying, and trying to believe in miracles.

"Please, God, bring her back." Rhys's life had been punctuated by losses — too many of them. First, his parents; then his rebel youngest brother, Easton.

Jacey was Easton's widow, and now she was married to Rhys's oldest brother, Luca. The two of them had thumbed their noses at the feud between their families and somehow found healing and love in the midst of tragedy. Rhys hadn't found any such thing. All he knew for sure right now was that he wasn't prepared to say goodbye to Alora Maddox.

He bowed his head over her hand. "It's too soon, God. I'm begging you."

⟨⟩

TITUS RAND STOOD outside Alora's curtained-off alcove in the intensive care unit, enduring each flirtatious glance and throaty greeting from the nurses. One perfume-scented nurse walked past him exactly twelve times. He counted, because noticing things was part of his job. Although he was mildly amused by her not-so-subtle attempts at catching his attention, he wasn't in the position to flirt. There was no room in his life for anything but work. He was too busy focusing on his most obvious mission — keeping CEO Alora Maddox alive and safe — as well as his less obvious mission of researching Rhys Calcagni's company on behalf of his other top-secret employer.

They'd sent him to scope out the viability of hiring Genesis & Sons to spearhead the development of a new line of cyber technologies. DRAW Corporation was the other think tank he'd been tasked to look into, if Genesis did not live up to its reputation at close scrutiny. Interestingly enough, Titus's under-cover role as Rhys's head of security was allowing him to investigate both companies at the same time.

He considered pulling his sunshades from his pocket to add an extra layer of insulation between him and the overly curious nursing staff, but that would require lifting his arm. The motorcycle ride in this morning had put more than enough strain on his injury already. The torn tendon was his souvenir for helping collar a pair of highly sought-after domestic terrorists at the airport upon his arrival into Anchorage. He'd successfully turned them over to the authorities, but not before the scumbags had worked in tandem to all but rip his arm from its socket.

That was nearly a month ago. Titus had iced the wound, dosed himself with pain killers, and maintained a self-prescribed physical therapy regimen to no avail. Apparently, this was an injury that wasn't going to heal on its own.

"My nurses don't mean any offense." The low, melodic voice provided a welcome interruption to the monotonous ache in Titus's arm.

"None taken." He spared a glance in the direction of the nurse's station. He'd already accepted the fact that working for billionaire Rhys Calcagni would forever be accompanied by scads of female attention. At least it wasn't accompanied by the usual flashing cameras here in the intensive care unit.

Only one woman remained behind the counter. She was looking down at her paperwork instead of directly at him, exuding the air of someone in charge. Probably a shift supervisor.

He eyed the curve of her neck, the perfect shell-shape of her ear, and the thick, dark mane of hair she'd drawn back in a tidy bun. She was a portrait of self-assurance and quiet efficiency, two traits he greatly admired.

"Most of the younger guests who make it to this part of the hospital come on a stretcher." A smile played around her glossy lips, one that didn't reach her eyes. "Other than that torn bicep tendon, however, you seem in pretty good shape." She finally looked up, arching her perfectly manicured brows in a challenge at him.

"Not much gets past you, eh?" He was impressed at her observation. Most women who'd walked by him the last fifteen minutes or so, probably hadn't noticed much besides his above-average height or the breadth of his shoulders. This woman, however, had noted the unnatural bulge of torn tendon beneath his suit jacket. If he had the time to pursue a personal attraction, this woman would have definitely made the cut.

"I'm a nurse." She returned to shuffling papers on the cabinet in front of her. "You should get your arm looked at. Most of those types of injuries don't heal on their own."

It was as if she'd been reading his thoughts. "So I've discovered." He grimaced. "I'm actually already scheduled for surgery." For security reasons, he didn't bother telling her it was this afternoon, nor did he bother informing her the procedure would take place in the same hospital he was standing in. He never volunteered details about himself, except on a need-to-know basis. Serving in undercover roles worked best when he avoided personal attachments. It would be a much easier rule of thumb to follow, if the nurse on the other side of the counter wasn't so blasted attractive. And fascinating. And...he drew in a slow, deep breath, willing his thoughts back to the job at hand.

She scanned his features and glanced away. "Glad to hear it. I'm sorry to butt in where I'm not needed." Her tone was casually impersonal.

What? He hoped his standoffishness hadn't offended her. That was never his intention. "Hey, I appreciate your concern." He did, too. In a world festering with crime and ugliness, he was quick to notice folks who bothered to spare a drop of human compassion for others.

"No problem." She picked up her stack of folders and, without saying another word, moved from behind the counter and glided down the hall in the opposite direction.

Titus allowed himself the one small luxury of following her graceful movements with his gaze. She was taller than average and built like an athlete. A volleyball player, maybe? Which meant he wouldn't completely dwarf her if they were standing face-to-face or...dancing.

Shoot! He forced his gaze away from the woman, knowing there would be no dancing dates in their future. *Guess I'm lonelier than I realized.* Or half out of his mind with pain. The meds he'd taken earlier weren't yet kicking in to his satisfaction.

He reached up with his good hand to turn up the volume on the earpiece in his right ear. Maybe getting back to his job of investigating the COO of Genesis & Sons would provide some modicum of distraction from his misery. Unfortunately, it necessitated a bit of eavesdropping. *Sorry, man. Just doing my job.*

What he overheard on the other side of the curtain made him go very still. He'd harbored some suspicions about the state of things between his newest employer and Alora Maddox, but this confirmed every last one of them and then some. Rhys Calcagni was head over heels in love with the CEO of his firm's biggest rival. Even more astounding, he was spending tens of thousands of dollars to ensure her safety without the knowledge of the other executives at either company.

Which made Rhys Calcagni *exactly* the caliber of man Titus Rand's other employer might be interested in working with.

CHAPTER 2: DREAMING DREAMS

ALORA

Alora felt like she was drowning in a sea of endless pain. Every cell in her body hurt — every bone and every muscle. To make matters worse, she seemed to be frozen in place, unable to move a muscle. Each time she reached the point where she thought she couldn't take it anymore, something cool and soothing would streak through her veins and carry her to a warmer, safer place. The pain would dim for a time, and she would float in a delicious pool of light.

However, the light always faded, and the pain always returned. Then she felt like she was drowning all over again.

The infinite cycle of pain and light continued on in a place that seemed to have no boundaries — no beginning or end, no day or night. The only disruption was the occasional babble of voices.

Worried voices. Sad voices. Pleading voices. Alora wished they would go someplace else and leave her to suffer in peace — all the voices except one, that is.

His voice. It was a deep, rich baritone that confided the kind of intimacies most women dreamed of hearing from their husbands or lovers. Like the other people who came and went from her presence, there was sadness and pleading in his tone. However, there was also adoration and hopeless longing — the kind that tugged at her heart and stayed with her long after his departure. Thankfully, he always returned. In fact, he was her most frequent visitor.

There was something vaguely familiar about him, though logic told her she couldn't possibly know the man. How could she? She wasn't dating anyone, much less married. In her line of work, she couldn't afford the luxury of too many personal and emotional attachments, though — at the moment — she couldn't remember what her line of work was, exactly.

Regardless, Alora didn't have a special someone in her life, which meant the romantic man talking to her and holding her hand must be a figment of her imagination. Or maybe she was dreaming. Which didn't keep her from looking forward to his visits, hating when each one came to an end, and missing him when he was gone.

"I need you to wake up, so I can make a proper fool of myself," he groaned softly.

To Alora's astonishment, she could understand every word he said this time. Sometimes the things people said to her were little more than a droning singsong in the distance. His words puzzled her, too. *Am I sleeping, then? But no. I can't be sleeping, because I can feel so much.* Cool sheets and soft blankets. Light pressure bearing down on the lower half of her face. And pain — the constant pain.

The man picked up her hand to caress her fingers. His touch was always so achingly gentle. And warm — toasty warm — so warm that she wished she could shrink herself down and curl her entire body inside his hand. She could also feel the brush of warm metal on his pinky finger. If she had to venture a guess, he was wearing some sort of signet ring.

After a while, he pressed her fingers to his lips and kissed each one. His mouth was firm and possessive, cherishing and (again) deliciously warm. *Who are you?* She wanted so desperately to know his name. *How do I know you? What are you to me?*

"Come back to me," he pleaded in a voice barely above a whisper. He sounded like somebody important to her, someone who cared — deeply and intimately — making her wish he was real and that the moment they were sharing was actually happening.

Am I dreaming? If I am, then why can't I wake

up? Dream or not, she wanted to answer the man, to open her eyes and say something reassuring, but it became suddenly clear that task wasn't going to be an easy one. *I am awake, so why can't I open my eyes?* She tried again without success. *What is wrong with me?* Her body felt strangely weak, and her limbs refused to respond to the command of her brain.

"I know you're still in there, Alora, and I'm going to find a way to bring you back."

The man's half-crooning, half-pleading voice made her insides melt with wonder. In the past, she'd dreamed of meeting a man who would say wonderfully romantic things to her. A man who made her feel special, someone who saw more than her wealth and family name, someone who saw the real her — the woman beneath it all. In her experience, most men who flirted with her did so simply because they wanted something from her — a solution to a problem, a negotiation that would result in a business transaction, because... Her mind raced. *Because I manage things. I delegate. I lead.*

"Can you hear me, Alora?" The man's voice changed. A note of excitement crept into it. "Call me crazy, but it feels like you can." His voice sounded closer as if he was leaning in her direction. "If you can hear me, babe, I want you to know everything is going to be alright."

Babe. Alora's thoughts floated dreamily for a

moment over his use of the endearment. She adored the way his voice caressed each word, much the same way his hand was cradling hers.

"You were air-lifted to the hospital a few weeks ago, because you were involved in a car accident; but the doctor assures us you are healing."

Weeks! I've been in the hospital for weeks? Alarm welled in Alora's chest as the details of the accident shivered across her memory and took shape. She'd been behind the wheel of her Lamborghini when an enormous dump truck with tinted windows had come out of nowhere. The driver had gunned his accelerator straight for her. *He made no effort to avoid me!* Some nameless, faceless silhouette behind a wall of dark glass had tried to kill her and nearly succeeded.

She'd yanked her wheel at the last minute, narrowly avoiding a direct T-bone. However, her luxury sports car had been no match for the tank-sized rig that sideswiped her. She'd spun out of control and hit the guardrail so hard that her car flipped over it and hurtled down an embankment. She remembered the metallic taste of panic and the swift burst of realization that it was the end for her. Then her memories blurred.

I'm alive, though. Somehow I lived through it. Alora struggled to remember more leading up to the accident and found that she could finally do so. The more she remembered, the clearer her thoughts became. There'd been an important meeting she'd attended prior to getting in her car — a successful contract negotiation with a quality control firm based in New Hampshire. They'd sent their two top executives to meet with her, because... *I work at DRAW Corporation. I'm Alora Maddox, their freaking CEO!*

Her hand convulsed in excitement on the warm fingers laced through hers. *I'm alive and in the hospital! I survived!*

"Alora?" The man's fingers tightened on hers. "Did you just—? You did! I know you did!" He drew a deep breath before exclaiming, "Nurse? Somebody, call a nurse! I think she's waking up!"

CHAPTER 3: SEARCHING FOR ANSWERS

ALORA

One month later

A lora pressed her fingers lightly to the sides of her neck. It was wonderfully liberating to have the padded cervical collar removed at last. She'd worn it for so many weeks that she was beginning to fear it would permanently attach itself to her skin.

Her navy pinstriped suit looked much better without the oversized adornment hugging her throat, albeit her skin beneath it was a bit paler than usual. She could desperately use a few hours in the sun, regaining her normal pallor.

It wasn't simply vanity driving her desire to get back to looking and acting normal again, however. It was a necessity. As the newly installed CEO of DRAW Corporation, her job demanded that she present an image of authority, confidence, and strength. Others looked to her for direction. She planned to deliver.

"My next contract negotiation will be all the more fierce," she joked, peering into the mirror that the nurse handed her. "By losing the neck brace, I am forfeiting the sympathy vote of everyone I come in contact with." She was sitting on the edge of a paper-covered chair in a patient exam room of the hospital.

"Would you like to keep it, then?" the lovely dark-haired nurse grinned at her. "I can package it up all nice and pretty and send it home with you."

"I'll pass." Though Alora chuckled, the white and chrome room, along with its antiseptic scent, churned at the shadowy memories that had been haunting her ever since she awoke from her coma. She was still struggling to figure out how many of her memories from the last few weeks had been real and how many of them had simply been the product of dreams...or drug-induced hallucinations. Lord knew she'd been on a full cocktail of pain meds at the time.

She particularly wished to know if the wonderful man with the whispery baritone had been real. She closed her eyes; and, for a moment, she was back in the intensive care unit with his fingers entwined around hers. Was it truly possible to dream the same dream over and over again like she had?

"Are you alright, Miss Maddox?" the nurse inquired anxiously.

Alora's eyelids fluttered open. "Perfectly alright," she lied. There was no way to explain her sadness over not knowing if the man in her hazy memories was real or not. *Good heavens!* If she mentioned her fears aloud, she might actually earn herself a referral for a psych evaluation or counseling.

"I saw the way you closed your eyes. On a scale of one to ten, with ten being the worst, how much pain are you in right now, Miss Maddox?" The nurse was standing behind a computer mounted on a cart with wheels. She used her pen to point toward a poster on the wall, bearing a set of yellow cartoon expressions that indicated various pain levels.

"I'm about a two, I guess," Alora fibbed again. "Headache," she explained with a wry smile. In reality, she was closer to a four on the pain scale, maybe a five. Her head was pounding, and there was a twisty sort of pain in the middle of her back that was starting to wear on her nerves. However, it had been x-rayed twice since her release from the hospital. According to her radiologist, her fractured ribs were fusing nicely. It would simply take a while longer for all the internal muscular and other soft tissue damage to fully heal. Or so the doctor claimed...

The nurse typed a note into Alora's patient file.

"I wonder if you could help me with something." Maybe it was the pain talking, but Alora suddenly did not want to go another day without answers to the questions burning inside her ever since her discharge.

"Sure, hon. What is it?" the nurse replied cheerfully.

"Might I be allowed to pay a quick visit down to the intensive care unit? I'd like to deliver some thank-you notes to the nursing staff. I was there for the better part of three weeks, and, well, they were pretty amazing." Or so she'd been told. She'd been unconscious for most of her stay in the ICU.

The nurse shrugged. "They're pretty strict about visitation rules down there, but I'm about to go on break. If I escort you to the nurse's station, myself, you shouldn't have any issues."

"Thank you kindly." Alora's heartbeat quickened at the thought of finally facing her biggest fear. She wished she'd thought of paying the intensive care ward a visit sooner. Ever since her hospital stay, she'd been receiving frequent deliveries of flowers from a secret admirer. She was hoping against hope it wasn't just a coincidence — that it, instead, meant the dreamy man in her memories was real.

"Hey, no problem." The nurse smiled. "We aim to please around here." She reached behind her for the wall phone. Picking it up, she punched in a number on the key pad. "Hi. This is Nurse Turner from Family Medicine. Is Jolene Shore available? Yes, thanks." There was a pause. "Hi, Jolene!

Tabitha here. I have somebody in my exam room who's asking to see you. Is now a good time? I'm about to go on break, so I could bring her down there." She listened for a few seconds. "The lovely Alora Maddox would like to thank you in person for services rendered during her recent stay. Oh, you do?" She raised her brows and glanced curiously over at Alora. "I doubt she'd mind that at all. See you in a bit. Thanks!" She hung up the receiver. "As it happens, the head nurse in ICU is already on her way up here."

"Too easy."

"I've gotta get going, but she'll be here in two snaps." Nurse Turner reached for the door handle.

"Thank you. For everything." After a lifetime of having access to unlimited amounts of wealth and privilege, Alora found herself being humbly grateful for the little things lately — like being alive — and the nursing staff at the Gjoa Haven Medical Center had played a vital role in making that happen. It was not something she would ever forget. In fact, her mind was already racing over the possibilities of holding a charity event to benefit the hospital in some way. She'd talk it over with her siblings soon to have them weigh in on it.

The door to her exam room re-opened in less than five minutes.

Alora immediately recognized the tall woman with her hair pulled back in a dark, tidy bun. She had almond-shaped eyes — a striking shade of hazel, bordering on green — and a wide, expressive mouth that wasn't smiling.

"Thank you so much for coming to meet with me." Alora rose from the exam bench to hold out her hand.

Jolene Shore shook it with a cautious once-over, but immediately motioned Alora back to the exam table. "Please, take a seat."

"I'm tired of sitting," Alora admitted, returning to her perch.

"I'm not surprised." Jolene surveyed her with understanding in her assessing gaze. "You're accustomed to your independence, Miss Maddox, but what you've been through lately has short-circuited it."

"Please, call me Alora." Alora had never been big on pomp and posturing.

Jolene made a comical face and took a seat on the doctor's stool. She spun around in it to face Alora. "You're a CEO of a world-renowned company. I think you've earned the right to a title."

Alora gave a dry chuckle. "And you've seen me at my worst. Stripped of everything but a hospital gown and a few life-saving cords and tubes. If that doesn't put us on a first-name basis, nothing will." Being at the top was a lonely place. She didn't have many friends, but she liked what she saw in Jolene Shore.

"Very well, Alora. Tabitha said you wanted to thank me, but I assure you I was just doing my job." She shook her head, her expression sober. "On my ward, there are no haves and have-nots when it comes to patient care. We treat everyone the same — from dog mushers to state senators. We fight equally hard to save every life. My only wish is that we could," she sighed.

"Well, it sounds like you and your team performed miracles on my behalf," Alora noted softly. "Since I was one of the lucky ones who got to go home, please allow me to express my enormous gratitude for doing your job in such an exemplary way. No matter how you try to downplay it, you and your team saved my life." She appreciated the head nurse's humble attitude; but, from her perspective, the woman was an angel of mercy.

"Gratitude accepted." Jolene's expression finally relaxed into a semblance of a smile. "We had some help, though. There were lots of well wishes and prayers going up on your behalf the entire time. According to our logs, you weren't alone for a single minute during visiting hours."

Oh? Alora's interest piqued. This was the biggest reason she'd wanted to speak to Jolene Shore. "I assume my family visited?" This was only a partial truth. She knew for a fact her parents had been out of the country a good amount of her hospital stay, and the rest of her family had been juggling their jobs and regular lives. Jacey, who adored her, had flown to Nashville at least once to record a song.

Jolene made a huffing sound. "Family, friends, your entire team of hunky bodyguards..." She shook her head. "Some of my younger nurses could barely do their jobs when the tallest one was around. They swooned every time he showed up, though I don't think he paid much attention to any of us." Her tone held a shade of bitterness.

My entire team of hunky bodyguards, eh? Alora's insides turned a few flip-flops. None of this was sounding familiar, but she sensed she was close to learning something vital about what had happened while she was in the coma.

"Which one?" she asked in a casual tone. She flipped a handful of red-gold hair over her shoulder. "I'll have him fired at once!" she added with a teasing level of vehemence.

Jolene Shore shrugged. "Tall, broad, blue-black hair. Had a torn bicep tendon early on, but one of our surgeons fixed 'em up. I think I overheard Mr. Calcagni call him Titus a few times."

Titus. The name wasn't ringing a bell. Was he the guy who'd sat by her side and held her hand, then? "I presume the Mr. Calcagni you're referring to is my brother-in-law, Luca Calcagni?" It wasn't surprising that Luca would travel with a team of bodyguards. He'd majorly beefed up security measures ever since he'd married Jacey. He was shamelessly protective of her and her son, Race — his own nephew whom he'd formally adopted.

Jolene shook her head. "He was here several times, but I was actually referring to his brother, Mr. Rhys Calcagni. He visited quite a bit, too. So did Mr. Knox Calcagni."

Alora's eyes widened. *Rhys and Knox Calcagni?* That would mean all three Calcagni brothers had visited her, which made no sense! She knew very little about Knox, but she knew for sure that Rhys despised her. Correction. They despised each other. He was one of those insufferable, condescending jerks who thought he was better than everyone else.

Her lips tightened. He'd made that clear enough during their high school days. They'd had the misfortune to end up at a cotillion together, where they were forced to share a dance. Instead of the usual small-talk, they'd ended up arguing — not a surprise, considering he was a Calcagni, and she was a Maddox. It sort of came with the territory. Oddly enough, she had no recollection about exactly what they'd disagreed about. All she remembered was that he'd accused her of being shallow and manipulative. She'd ended the dance early and left him alone on the ballroom floor. They hadn't exchanged many words since.

It wasn't like they were uncivil to each other. They were too old for such pettiness. They simply avoided each other as much as possible. Their paths inevitably crossed on occasion, since his oldest brother was married to her youngest sister, but that was it.

"Did this Titus accompany Mr. Rhys Calcagni on most of his visits?" Alora felt like she was grasping at straws, trying to piece together the mystery of what had taken place in her bay while her eyes were closed. Her mind raced through the possible reasons for the presence of so many Calcagnis at the hospital — everything from corporate espionage attempts to... her mind drew a blank. *I have no idea.* It truly made no sense. Though she despised the Calcagnis on principle, it felt out of character for them to stoop so low.

"Every time," Jolene affirmed. She glanced suddenly at the closed door and lowered her voice. "Listen, I hope I'm not crossing a line, but I have some questions of my own about Titus."

"You do?" A tremulous chuckle escaped Alora. Well, that made two of them. She had questions about a lot of things right now.

"Yes. So...I used to date a guy in our security department, and we still talk sometimes even though it didn't work out." She glanced over her shoulder again before continuing. "Anyhow, he told me that Titus was one of many plain-clothes operatives crawling the place the whole time you were hospitalized. Right up until this conversation, I just assumed they were in your employ."

Alora gave a mirthless chuckle. "Maybe they are." She rolled her eyes. "Since I'm missing a few weeks of my life, I guess I'll have to ask my executive team." She was fairly certain the plain-clothes security men Jolene described were not, however, in the employ of the Maddoxes. The authorization for such a thing would have had to come from her parents or grandparents, none of whom seemed to understand how dangerous her brother, Kellan, was — or whoever his creepy look-alike truly was. She and her siblings suspected they were dealing with an imposter and were doing everything they could to track down the real Kellan Maddox. Meanwhile, their grandfather fawned to no end over the poser, treating him like his favorite grandchild.

Alora's thoughts roved back to the topic at hand. Her bodyguards. She did not doubt the mysterious and swoon-worthy Titus was in the employ of the Calcagnis. "How many security guys would you say there were?" she inquired in a low voice. Might as well pump Jolene for all the information she could while she had her undivided attention.

Jolene shrugged and glanced down at her watch. "A half dozen, maybe more? Matt said he was pretty sure they were pulling patrols both outside and inside. He swore they were even doing sweeps overhead." She rose from the stool. "I'm sorry I have to cut our visit short, but duty calls."

"Sweeps overhead?" Alora echoed, anxious to

glean as much information as possible from the woman before she departed.

"Yeah. Can you believe it?" Jolene scrunched her dark eyebrows. "By helicopter, no less. Everyone else thought it was the paparazzi, since we had a celebrity in our midst."

Alora stood and waved a disparaging hand. "Oh, stop, already!"

Jolene arched her dark brows. "Well, it's true. Technically, we had a bunch of celebrities coming and going, if you count all the Calcagnis and Maddoxes. It's totally against all hospital regs and privacy laws, but don't be surprised if you see some amateur cell phone pics pop up on social media in the coming days. I'm sorry, Alora, truly sorry," she shook her head, "but it's the price of being famous."

Alora chuckled. "If you say so." She'd been raised as a Maddox, so she was accustomed to being in the spotlight. Their public relations department at DRAW Corporation would handle anything that got out of control — copyright-wise or otherwise. Their PR team was likely already sending take-down notices to dozens of online social rags. "Well, thank you for your time, Jolene. I really appreciate everything you've done for me. I know you're not supposed to accept gifts, but—"

"There is something you can do for me, if you're asking." Jolene paused in her trek to the door and half-turned back to Alora. For the first time during their encounter, she seemed uncertain.

"Sure. Anything legal." Alora softened the warning with another chuckle. "Actually, I'd love to cater in a lunch for your whole department. Just name the date and restaurant."

Jolene's lips twitched. "Lunch would be really nice. Any time or any place of your choice. We're not picky down in the ICU. However...ah, never mind." She shook her head. "Seriously, lunch would be great."

"What else?" Alora demanded, rising to her feet. "You were about to say something. I know you were."

"It's nothing, really," Jolene sighed.

"Okay. So it shouldn't be a big deal to repeat it, then."

Jolene bit her lower lip. "It's truly silly. I was just going to say, if you ever run into Titus, I'd like to know if he's okay. His arm was messed up pretty badly."

"I will." Alora suddenly wondered if she and the lovely nurse were crushing on the same man.

"Thanks, Alora. I'd appreciate it. You don't need to tell him I asked about him or anything." Jolene reached the door and turned the knob.

"Did Titus ever come into the sick bay with me?" Alora asked suddenly. She was still desperate to discover anything that would shed light on the mysterious man in her dreams.

"No." The nurse's voice was emphatic. "He always stood guard outside the curtained-off area. Only your family and the Calcagnis went in to see you."

I see. Alora's heart sank. Maybe the man in her dreams didn't exist, after all. Maybe her new secret admirer was a mere coincidence. A new hire, from any number of the departments employed by DRAW, who had a crush on her. Heck, he could be some creepy stalker, for all she knew.

"Well, it was nice talking to you, Jolene." On impulse, Alora dug in her purse for a business card. "Here. You should probably have my number, since we're planning a lunch date for your department."

Jolene looked a little awed at the gold-mono-grammed card. "Wow! Thanks." She pocketed it. "My nurses are going to be thrilled when they hear about the lunch."

"Fantastic! I'll be in touch." Alora glided from the room after Jolene, anxious to return to her office to start digging into who Titus was and what his affil-iations were. Her gold stilettos clacked against the white tile floors of the long hospital hallway as she made her way to the elevators.

Right before the elevator doors closed, a tall man in gray jogging pants and a navy hoodie eased himself inside the elevator. The brim of a ball cap shaded his eyes, and his head remained lowered.

It wasn't until he leaned forward to mash the

down arrow that Alora noticed his left arm was in a sling. Her heart skipped a few beats. She peered at him from beneath her lashes and noted that his hair was so black and shiny it almost appeared to glow blue beneath the fluorescent lighting. Could this be the mysterious Titus that Jolene had been telling her about? If so, there was a good chance he was following her!

One way to find out. Maybe it was risky, considering she had no idea who the man was and what his intentions were toward her, but she glanced up and looked directly at him. "Torn bicep, huh?"

He slowly raised his head to meet her gaze. "Good guess." His voice held a note of irony. "Are you a nurse?"

"You know I am not." She held his gaze without blinking. "Why are you following me, Titus?"

A grudging light of approval flashed in his dark, assessing eyes. "That sounded a lot like an accusation."

"I could have you arrested, you know," she taunted, just to see his reaction.

"For what?" he scoffed. "Last time I checked, arrests were accompanied by the burden of proof."

"I have witnesses. According to the nurse I just spoke with, you stood guard outside my bay in the ICU."

"Gee, you make me sound like such a bad guy."

The elevator came to a stop on the main level. The door made a dinging sound and rolled open.

"This isn't funny." Her lips trembled as she struggled to hold in a chuckle. "I'm in the middle of a serious interrogation here."

He motioned for her to step out ahead of him. "So I gathered." Eyes twinkling, he held his hand against the door to keep it from moving while she swept past him.

They stared at each other outside the elevator for several tense seconds., then both started laughing at the same time.

"There's a nurse named Jolene Shore in ICU who would like to know if your arm is okay."

His jaw tightened as he glanced down at his sling. "Tell her I'm on the mend."

Alora sensed there was more of a story there. "You should tell her yourself."

When he didn't answer, she teased, "Let me guess. I probably wouldn't want to see how the other guy looks, huh?"

"Guys," he corrected, arching a brow at her. "I was jumped by two of them."

"Sounds like you've had the time to come up with a pretty good story and everything. I'm impressed." Alora hitched her handbag strap higher on her shoulder and winced as the movement sent a strange twinge of pain through her middle back. "Hope you at least managed to give 'em a black eye."

"They're in jail." He cocked his head in concern at her. "You okay over there?"

She grimaced. "I'm on the road to recovery." A crazy long road that seemed to stretch on forever some days. She tapped her freshly lacquered nails against the sleeve of her suit. "Who do you work for?"

"That's need-to-know."

"Why did he hire you?"

"I didn't say my employer was a man."

She wrinkled her nose at him. "Are you always this difficult?"

"Only on Tuesdays," he shot back in a light tone. Then he sobered. "Now that we've met, I don't mind telling you that I intend to follow you on my motorcycle to wherever you're going, just like I followed you here to the hospital. For your safety, of course."

She huffed out a breath and started walking. It came as no surprise when he fell in step beside her. "You're in a sling. How can you possibly expect to provide security for me on the highway, while you're down an arm?"

"Because there will be an unmarked armored vehicle on either side of your Land Rover, and a helicopter flying point. I'm just along for the ride."

Her lips parted in shock. "You're kidding!" That was an awful lot of security for a single corporate CEO.

He raised his brows. "They were there earlier.

You just didn't notice them. But now that we've met, I don't see any reason to make the boys keep hiding themselves from you."

"Now that we've met, huh?" She made a face at him. "Something tells me our meeting was more than chance."

"I've been told you're a brilliant woman."

"Why are you doing this?" she sighed. "Really, Titus?"

"As I said, it's to keep you safe."

"Meaning you know about my brother's death wish for me." Her knees felt weak just talking about it. She struggled to force the memories of the car accident from her mind before she started hyperventilating.

"You don't really think he's your brother, do you?"

The concern and compassion in Titus's gaze was nearly her undoing. "I don't, and that terrifies me." Tears stung the backs of her eyelids. "Unfortunately, I've been so focused on trying to run a company without being able to turn my neck, that I haven't given my search for Kellan half the effort he deserves." Her head was pounding again, and her stomach was twisting in knots.

They paused beside her SUV, and she clicked her remote control to unlock it.

Titus reached around her to open the door for her. "I don't want to get your hopes up," he announced in a hushed voice, "but I may have a lead on the whereabouts of the real Kellan Maddox."

A sob tore from deep within her chest, and her knees nearly gave out.

His good hand shot out and steadied her elbow. "Get in, Alora." He gently guided her as she climbed into her driver's seat.

"You've got to give me more than that," she begged, gripping the steering wheel with both hands. Tears ran unchecked down her face.

"It's just a lead, but my employer flew there to follow up on it yesterday. We have reason to believe your brother may have been involved in a yacht accident. If that is true, he was taken to a small hospital near La Rochelle, where a patient meeting his description is being treated for head trauma."

Alora's whole body shook with a mixture of relief and weakness. She wept silently for several moments before she could collect herself enough to respond. "The next time you see your employer, please tell him I want to thank him." She drew a shuddering breath. "In person."

"I will."

"I want to know something else." She stared straight ahead. "Is he the one who held my hand in the hospital?"

Titus was silent for so long that she didn't think he intended to answer her.

"I need to know," she pressed in a shaky voice. She felt close to cracking.

"Yes."

She leaned back weakly against the captain's seat. "So he's real." More tears dripped down her cheeks. Her relief was profound.

"I have every reason to believe so," he joked.

"I'm not sure I would have survived my coma without him," she whispered, closing her eyes. Throughout the past month, she'd found she could best re-live her memories of him when her eyes were closed. "I had one of those out-of-body experiences." She opened her eyes and blinked damply at Titus. "You know...the whole floating-toward-the-white-light thing. His voice called me back."

Titus reached inside the car to pat her hand on the steering wheel. "I'll be sure to tell my employer that, too. He'll be glad to know."

"Why all the secrecy?" she asked suddenly. *Who in the world required that level of subterfuge, and why?*

"He has his reasons, Alora. Trust me."

"He can't hide from me forever, Titus."

"He knows that."

CHAPTER 4: A MAJOR DISCOVERY

RHYS

Don Kappleman agreed to fly with Rhys to France in Rhys's private jet. Don was Luca's former man-of-everything as well as the new CEO of his recently acquired marketing firm, Titan Industries.

"How's the new biz?" Rhys asked, once they reached cruising altitude, allowing him to turn on the automatic pilot feature. He glanced over at his co-pilot, who was lounged comfortably in his seat, sipping on a chilled bottle of tea.

Don was a hulk of a man, taller than Rhys, and stacked like a bodybuilder. He kept the sides of his head closely shaved, a throwback to his special forces days, and a thin scar ran from the corner of his left eye to his ear.

He shrugged his massive shoulders and took another swig of his tea. "Still figuring it out. I would have crashed and burned already if it wasn't for Luca advising me."

"Luca's particularly skilled at keeping company's afloat." Rhys nodded. It wasn't the first buyout his oldest brother had overseen. Not even close. "You're in good hands." Family meant everything to Luca. There wasn't much he wouldn't do to help out a family member, and Don was more like a brother to him than a former employee. Plus, Don had real family ties to the Calcagnis, these days, now that he was married to Jacey's next older sister, Bailey.

"That I am." Don sounded grateful. His company held an exclusive contract with DRAW Corporation to handle the marketing leg of their business, which was the whole reason he'd acquired the firm. He'd immediately named his wife Executive Vice President, so she could personally manage the contract with DRAW. It was roughly the same position Bailey had held at DRAW, before her brother's imposter had outsourced it to Titan in the attempt to ruin her.

And now Rhys and Don were traveling to France to locate the real Kellan, so they could put an end to the imposter's shenanigans, once and for all.

"Have you made any progress yet on your plans to land a date with Alora?" Don's voice turned sly.

Very few people in the world knew about Rhys's feelings concerning the CEO of DRAW Corporation. Don was one of those people. Rhys idly fiddled with one of the controls on the panel in front of him, feeling foolish. "I've sent her roses."

"Oh, yeah?"

"A dozen or more times."

His friend chuckled. "You haven't told her yet, have you?"

"No."

"When are you—?"

"Soon," Rhys growled.

"Okay, okay!" Don held up his hands, making his tea slosh in its bottle.

Rhys didn't know why facing Alora was so hard after all the promises he'd made to himself at her hospital bedside — starting with his vow to finally tell her how he felt about her when she finally awoke.

Yet a whole month had passed since she'd awakened from her coma, and here he was — still playing the part of her secret admirer from a safe distance. His phone screen flashed with an incoming message.

It was from Titus Rand. Rhys hastily read what his head of security had to say and grew still.

It's time to tell her, sir. She's starting to put the pieces together.

That meant Alora had discovered Titus was shadowing her. Rhys breathed deeply and started to type. *I will. Tomorrow.* There. He'd committed to the decision, and he never went back on his word. That didn't keep his stomach from tightening at the prospect, though, of putting himself out there to be rejected, once and for all. His cowardice all these years had allowed him to continue hoping. And now that hope might be stripped away from him forever.

His screen flashed with three dots to indicate Titus was typing again. *She wants to meet the man who held her hand. Near-death experience. Says you called her back and wants to thank you — personally.*

Really? Wow! A ribbon of hope sliced itself through Rhys's chest. *Maybe I have a chance with her, after all.*

THERE WAS no mistaking the fact that the man Rhys and Don found in the hospital near La Rochelle was the missing Kellan Maddox — the *real* Kellan, though he was groggily recovering from a traumatic head injury and had no clear idea who he was. It took several hours to settle his medical expenses with the French hospital via a series of wire transfers, but Rhys prevailed. Before nightfall, they were back on his jet, this time with Kellan in the care of a registered nurse, who agreed to accompany them for an exorbitant fee and a return ticket home.

By the wee hours of the morning, Rhys and Don had Kellan safely checked in at the Gjoa Haven Medical Center. Through much negotiating, they managed to secure a private room for him with Titus Rand standing guard outside his door.

Then came the hard part of Rhys's job — notifying Kellan's family, though he knew it would likely blow his cover as Alora's secret admirer. He had gone to extraordinary measures, and a great deal of expense, to bring her brother home; and he'd done it for one reason only. Love. Love for a woman who'd barely acknowledged his existence up to this point. Love for a woman who despised him, his family, and everything they represented as her biggest corporate rival.

Bracing himself for the personal emotional fallout that was sure to follow, Rhys summoned Kellan's siblings via the same group message their inner circle had used to communicate while Alora was lying in a coma. Both Bailey's and Jacey's husbands were included in the group chat thread, along with Knox Calcagni and Bailey's office manager, Priscilla — basically all the offspring of both feuding families. It was an odd alliance that the rest of the world was not yet aware of. The elder leadership at their rival companies would come unglued if they ever got wind of it.

The Maddox siblings' response to Rhys's earth-shattering news was swift and astounding. They thanked him profusely but insisted that they, alone, would reunite with their brother. They wished for no one else to learn about the real Kellan's return —

not the rest of their family, their company employees, the paparazzi, or the law — until they determined how they were going to handle the imposter who had nearly destroyed their lives.

Rhys was puzzled. He'd expected them to immediately have the imposter arrested for his brutal attempt on Alora's life. That's what he would have done. It's what he wanted to do right now; he had all the pieces in place to make it happen. He was livid at the thought of the heinous creep spending another moment in freedom instead of behind bars where he belonged. The only thing that held him back was a message from Alora. His heart pounded when he noticed that she had messaged him directly.

Please don't call the police yet. I have a plan.

Of course she did. His lips tightened at her thinly veiled attempt to take control of the situation. He should have expected it. A Maddox would never take their marching orders from a hated Calcagni. Which didn't change the fact they were dealing with the actions of a heinous criminal here.

Blood boiling as he braced for their coming confrontation, he typed back. *Give me one good reason. He tried to kill you.*

She responded seconds later. *I will. In person.*

Rhys had no idea what she could possibly say to him that would change his mind about calling the law, but it felt unreasonable to deny her such a simple request.

By the time visiting hours at the hospital rolled around, Jacey, Bailey, Alora, and Greyson were assembled in the parking garage — ready to walk inside together. Thanks to Titus Rand and his associates working in conjunction with hospital security, the siblings were allowed to enter through a restricted access area to avoid attracting too much attention. Luca and Don accompanied their wives.

Rhys led them to Kellan's room, with a variety of curious stares burning a hole in his shoulder blades, not the least of which was Alora's gaze. He was anxious to have their promised moment alone, but it appeared she had every intention of seeing her brother first.

He threw open the door to Kellan's room and ushered the entire group in ahead of him. They rushed forward to form a semi-circle around his bed. A hushed silence settled, while Rhys closed the door and remained standing discreetly to one side.

"Welcome home, Kellan." Alora's voice shook with so much emotion that Rhys longed to go stand beside her. He missed the many hours he'd gotten to spend holding her hand and the way her hand had fit so perfectly in his. He wondered if she would ever allow him to do so again, now that she was fast figuring out his role in all this.

Just being in the same room with her again was doing crazy things to his heart, which was pounding erratically. He couldn't take his eyes off her and was grateful her attention was currently focused on her brother.

She was wearing a gray skirt and blazer this morning with a hint of oceanic tones that brought out the sea-blue of her eyes. Her red-gold hair, that she usually wore down, was twisted in a loose up-do. Pearls glistened in her ears, and a pearl choker rode her delicate throat.

She was the first to enclose Kellan in her arms, as he slowly sat up in bed and stared at those gathered around him. "Alora?" He looked tired and dazed, his auburn hair twisting and waving wildly in all directions. "Jace?" He blinked a few times. "What happened? Where am I?"

It was like watching a miracle take place. Rhys's shoulders relaxed at the knowledge that Kellan was finally remembering. His French doctor had warned it would take time, though he'd been unable to give any precise projections. He claimed Kellan's head injuries were so extensive he might never fully regain his memories. Fortunately, he was wrong.

"You were in a yacht accident off the coast of France." Greyson reached up to straighten his maroon bowtie which was askew as always. As the techno-genius of the family, he'd always impressed Rhys as a bit on the eccentric side. His hair was only moderately better arranged than his brother's, though he'd never suffered any medical catastrophes that Rhys was aware of.

Tears rolled unashamedly down Greyson's lightly freckled features. "And now you're home." He shot a grateful glance in Rhys's direction. They hadn't had a chance to speak yet, but Rhys knew that was coming.

Bailey was wrapped in her husband's embrace, weeping silently against Don's broad shoulder. He cradled her close, making Rhys taste envy. What he wouldn't give to hold Alora that way...to have the right to hold her that way.

Without warning, she glanced in his direction.

Their gazes clashed and held for a breathless moment. Her sea-blue eyes sought answers for things he prayed he was prepared to explain to her satisfaction.

He knew it was a shock for her to absorb everything that had hit her in recent months — her ascent to CEO at her company, the discovery that she and her siblings were adopted, her realization that the man currently serving in Kellan's shoes at her firm was an imposter, the knowledge that her real brother had been missing for months, her near-fatal car accident, and now the fact that a man employed by her greatest corporate rival harbored romantic feelings for her.

She lowered her gaze, leaving Rhys feeling bereft again.

She addressed her brother. "We're going to get you all the help you need to ensure your full recovery." She swayed a little in her impossibly high heels as she spoke.

Rhys took a few steps in her direction.

"Why? Am I sick?" Kellan's pale features were puzzled and anxious. He looked a little lost amidst the tumble of white sheets and blankets.

"You suffered a head injury," she replied softly, leaning over to lightly tweak one of his big toes through the sheets and blankets. "That's why it took you so long to remember us."

A lopsided smile played around his lips. "Not entirely true. I never forgot your faces. I just couldn't remember your names or much of anything else." His brow wrinkled as he pondered their expressions. "At least not anything important. I only remembered odds and ends, like how much I miss eating caviar."

"Gross!" Jacey pretended to shudder, though her blue eyes were misty with unshed tears.

"Oh, stop already," he chided good naturedly. "Not everyone can survive on turnips and weedy things." It was a dig at the fact she was a health nut with a somewhat recent leaning toward becoming a full-fledged vegan.

The siblings enjoyed about an hour of reuniting before Kellan started to doze off. A doctor entered the room to examine him, and his family scattered after agreeing to reconvene in the same place, come dinner time. Soon the doctor made his exit, leaving Alora and Rhys alone with the sleeping Kellan.

Rhys finally allowed himself the luxury of approaching her. They stood side-by-side for an extended moment, with him hardly daring to look at her. He had no idea how to begin explaining his complicated position. He finally settled for following his instincts and reached for her hand.

Her breathing hitched audibly, but her fingers closed around his.

It was quite possibly his finest moment. Time could have stopped right there, and he would have forever been happy.

"May I take you to lunch?" It wasn't the perfect start to any of the conversations he'd practiced in his head, but it was the first thing that came out of his mouth. *So lame.* At least he'd kept his promise to himself and finally asked her out. *Preparing to have my knees shot out from under me...*

"Where?"

It wasn't a no. His heart pounded a crazy rhythm. "Not too far." He knew she wouldn't want to leave her brother for long.

A soft sigh escaped her. "This is complicated, isn't it?" She glanced down at their joined hands. "Us. We're complicated."

Us. Joy flooded his chest at the realization that she was speaking in plurals. In his wildest dreams, he'd never expected such acceptance, and certainly not such quick capitulation. "I never expected it to be easy." His fingers curled more firmly around hers, and still she did not pull back. "Nothing worth having ever comes easy." *Not even to a billionaire.* Falling in love was the great equalizer. It made every man vulnerable, no matter the size of his bank accounts.

She made another soft sound. "I wanted so badly for you to be real...the man holding my hand back in the ICU, that is. Until I met Titus in the elevator, I'd just about convinced myself you weren't real." After a pause, she added quietly, "Of all the people you could have been, it wasn't supposed to be you."

His heart sank. "You mean I wasn't supposed to be a Calcagni."

"Yes."

"I've never seen you duck from a challenge," he assured, rubbing his thumb over the top of her hand. "You always were a fighter." *It's what kept you alive.*

To his dismay, she shook her head. "I used to think I was, but I gave up in there, Rhys. While I was lying in a coma, I was in so much pain. So afraid. So utterly defeated. One day I let go and started floating toward a bright light. The pain started to fade. It was a welcome feeling." She tipped her face up to his, her blue gaze tormented. "I think on some level, I realized I was going to a place where there's no coming back from, but I was so ready to end the pain. Willing to do whatever it took to leave it behind."

Rhys pivoted to face her. He reached out to ever-so-lightly cup her cheek. "But you survived even that."

"No. I didn't." A sheen of tears made her eyes glisten like blue diamonds. "I was truly dying. It was a voice that stopped me from leaving. I could have sworn I heard a man begging me to come back. Was it you?"

"Does it matter?"

"To me it does."

"You're relentless." He glanced away from her, lowering his hand from her cheek. "Something tells me I'm not going to have any pride left by the time you're finished with me."

"Is that a yes?"

"I prayed, yes. I begged God to spare you, and I begged you to keep fighting."

"You saved my life, Rhys. Then you brought my brother home. You've done more for me and my family than we can ever repay."

He grimaced. "Good thing I'm not looking for payment. Although, I wouldn't mind you saying yes to my offer to take you to lunch."

"Yes to lunch," she said quickly.

"Thank you." He smiled and reached for her other hand. They stood facing each other, hands clasped, at the foot of Kellan's bed.

"Just let me finish saying what I have to say first, okay?"

He nodded, blissfully content to gaze at her and listen to her for as long as she needed him to.

"I'm trying to understand why, Rhys." Her perfect brow wrinkled in contemplation as she regarded him. "Despite being surrounded by wealth and privilege most of my life, no one has ever fought for me the way you did. You didn't just spend money on me. You spent time and energy. You prayed. You cared. You gave yourself. No one — and I mean no one — has ever done anything like that for me."

It tore at Rhys's heart to know she was telling the truth. He understood how lonely it could be at the top of the corporate ladder, but at least he'd always had a loving family to share his successes with. Alora, on the other hand, came from such a disjointed home and company, that she'd truly been alone — until now.

"Well, now you can't make that claim anymore," he said softly.

"Yes, and I don't know what to do about it," she cried in a low voice, squeezing his hands.

"How about we start with lunch?"

She looked close to weeping. "Where could we possibly go, Rhys? What could we possibly do that would escape the notice of the paparazzi, thereby avoiding a fallout of nuclear proportions with both our families?"

He waggled his brows at her. "It's just lunch, Alora."

"It's not just lunch, and you know it. It's—" She shook her head, looking like she was struggling to find the right words.

"Worth it." He narrowed his gaze on her. "At least to me it is. You're worth every risk I'm going to have to take to keep you in my life." *Please say I'm worth it to you in return.*

"But we can't afford to be seen together like this. Not until the matter of Kellan's imposter is settled, at any rate. I can't give my family any reason to use their influence with the board to unseat me." She bit her lower lip. "Because that would leave my siblings — all of them, except Jacey — at the complete mercy of an imposter."

"Who you could have arrested within the hour," he reminded, using their joined hands to tug her closer. "All you have to do is pick up the phone. Your proof is lying there in that bed." He angled his head in Kellan's direction.

"It's too soon," she protested. "We still don't know who this imposter is, what he wants, or why he targeted my brother."

"Money, most likely," Rhys pointed out bluntly. "Kellan was an easy target, because he's rich and they happen to look a lot alike."

"So much that it's uncanny," she agreed with a shiver.

"Not to mention Kellan had no memory of who

he was after his accident. It was the perfect opportunity for a criminal."

She nodded. "My brother's imposter puts on a flawless act, too. He knows so much about Kellan that it's downright terrifying. His stories go back to Kellan's childhood."

Rhys shrugged. "There's a lot about your family in the press. He must have studied you. Really done his homework."

"A little too well." She shuddered. "It wasn't easy, but I managed to get some of the imposter's DNA samples and fingerprints to Titus yesterday. I'm hoping to hear back from him really soon."

"Look at you!" Rhys grinned down at her. "Tapping like a pro into the resources of the security firm I hired to protect you."

She blushed. "I don't even want to know how much you've spent on saving my life and Kellan's."

"You're worth every penny," he assured, drawing her closer. It was the most wonderful feeling in the world to know that he finally had a shot at dating Alora Maddox — or so he hoped.

"Rhys," she exclaimed softly. "Don't get me wrong..."

"But," he sighed, bracing himself for a let-down. His shot at dating her felt suddenly fleeting.

"You're everything I ever dreamed of in a relationship, except for—"

"My last name," he growled. "I know. You keep reminding me."

"I'm sorry! It's so unfair to you, but it's true. We can't pretend like it doesn't matter."

"So you're agreeing to go to lunch with me, so long as we're not seen together?" he mused.

"Yes." She gave a nervous-sounding chuckle. "After all you've done for me, you deserve so much better than this, but that's what we have to work with."

His gaze fell to her lush lips, and he longed to kiss away her fears. "I think I did a pretty good job of playing the part of your secret admirer the past few weeks. I could continue in that role." *I will happily continue in that role. I think I've proven that I'll do whatever it takes to keep you in my life.*

She scanned his features anxiously. "You would do that for me?"

He huffed out a short laugh. "You really feel the need to ask?"

"Then, yes. To lunch. To...us."

It was all Rhys needed to hear. He bent his head to claim her lips.

CHAPTER 5: NOT SO SECRET CONVERSATIONS

ALORA

Rhys's warm, firm mouth moved against Alora's, making her want to laugh and cry at the same time. This was the man who'd held her hand during her darkest hours. The man who'd stood by her in ways no one else ever had. It was breath-stealing and heart-shaking to realize she'd inspired the loyalty and devotion of someone who might actually stand a chance of protecting her from all the dangers headed her way.

Correction. He was already protecting her, he'd been protecting her, and he would continue to do so. A Calcagni, no less. A man who was supposed to be her enemy and rival. It was mind boggling and utterly entrancing.

Oh, how wrong she'd been about him, thinking he was just another egotistical rich jerk! Yes, he was diabolically clever, a number-crunching genius, and a man who pursued what he wanted with unwavering intent. But he'd used all that incredible brain power of his to save her life — not to harm it, her company, or anyone in her family. She'd been perfect for the plucking, a sitting duck for corporate sabotage, but all he'd done when she was at her most vulnerable was to spread his eagle wings to protect her.

There was no logical explanation for such unselfish charity, other than... Her breath clogged in her throat as the truth struck her. Rhys Calcagni wasn't just attracted to her. He didn't find her to be pretty or just fancy taking her out to lunch for her engaging conversation abilities or charismatic company. It was more than that. He could recount in sordid detail the rocky history between their companies. He knew her family's darkest secrets. He didn't need her money or want her job. There was not a blessed reason for him to choose her over any other single, datable woman unless...

He truly cares for me!

Butterflies swarmed inside her stomach. Unfortunately, that discovery wasn't something the world could know about just yet.

She broke off their kiss, pressed her palms to his chest to give him a gentle push, and took a step back.

Rhys's arms returned to his sides, and he

regarded her with heavy-lidded, male satisfaction. A girl could drown in those eyes. They were the color of a rich, aged bourbon.

"Rhys, we can't, just..." Her voice was low and shaky. "I mean, someone might..." She caught her lower lip between her teeth in agitation, glancing hastily around them. To her enormous relief, Kellan was still asleep, and the door to his room was still shut. Her brother's safety might very well depend on her and Rhys's discretion in the coming days. They would be wise to remember it.

"It's okay." He assured softly. "Titus is on the other side of the door. No one will get past him without me knowing."

Well, what about Kellan? Alora couldn't remember ever feeling this off balance. She smoothed a hand over her loose up-do and shot another hasty glance at her brother. "If he wakes up soon, we're going to have a lot of explaining to do."

"There is that." Rhys didn't sound half as worried as she felt. In fact, he didn't look worried at all. He simply looked a bazillion shades of gorgeous, wealthy, and powerful in his designer black suit and dress shoes.

Alora felt a blush coming on at the memory of her hands resting briefly on his chest. It was clear that the tall, slim, number-crunching COO of Genesis & Sons was no stranger to the gym. Beneath his immaculately pressed shirts was a very hard, very sculpted set of pecs.

While her brain slowly turned to mush, he treated her to a faint smile. "Titus will be happy to escort you to lunch."

Of course he will. She still had no idea where they were going. "Thank you, Rhys. For everything." She smiled ruefully at the knowledge that Titus hadn't likely let her stray far from his sight since her car accident.

"I'll see you soon." Rhys strode to the door and let himself out.

Alora wrapped her arms around her middle, feeling suddenly bereft. She pivoted to face her brother's hospital bed. He was lying too still, his breathing too shallow to escape her suspicions. "You can quit pretending to be asleep now."

Kellan cracked one eyelid open and grinned. "You know me so well."

She rolled her eyes at him. "So was that whole tired act back there for the benefit of our other siblings, or what?"

"I wish." He grunted, turning sober. "These dizzy spells come and go, leaving me feeling as useless as a sack of potatoes."

His face was much paler than she remembered, and way too thin. The lines in his face were sharper, and the shadows beneath his eyes smudged with purple, giving lie to his claim he wasn't tired.

"You love potatoes," she pointed out, hoping to distract him from his moping.

"And, apparently, you love Rhys Calcagni," he shot back, grimacing as he pushed himself to a sitting position. He shoved a hand through his auburn hair, ruffling it. The fact that he made no effort to smooth it back in place worried her to no end. In the past, he'd been far more concerned about his appearance than all her other siblings put together — a debonair ladies' man to a fault.

"I..." Alora blushed at his accusation and was momentarily at a loss for words. His full frontal attack was as unexpected as his ruffled appearance. She couldn't define or quantify what had just happened between her and Rhys, so there was no point in trying. His kisses still had her mind spinning and her heart doing backflips.

"It's okay. Your secret's safe with me," her brother informed her cheerfully. "You could have done worse than him. Just saying." He eyed her expression. "A lot worse. Pardon me for pointing this out, but highly successful people like you are notorious for making poor personal choices."

"What in heaven's name are you talking about?" she spluttered. It wasn't like she never dated. She went out with guys...once in a blue moon.

"You're married to your job, sis. Everyone but you seems to know that, which doesn't leave you much time for playing the field. You know...to weed out the frogs from the princes."

"But he's a Calcagni," she moaned, closing her eyes again. *This will never work, not in a million bazillion years. What am I going to do about him? About us?* She blushed at the realization that she was already thinking in plurals.

"Yeah, I kinda picked up on that detail all on my own." Kellan's voice was affectionately sarcastic. "Even so, I meant what I said. A year ago, I would have called him names and used my superior dating experience to coach you on the many creatives ways you could break things off with him."

Her eyelids shot open. "Superior, eh?"

He pretended to flex his muscles, which was many shades of hilarious, given the fact he was wearing a hospital gown.

They both laughed at his antics. "Way superior. I could engineer a break up that would cause maximum humiliation and damage, but I won't. Not to him. As much as I hate to admit this about anyone bearing the last name of Calcagni, he's one of the good ones, sis."

She couldn't argue the point, since she'd experienced Rhys's extraordinary brand of benevolence up close and personal. "Et tu, Brute?" she teased.

"Hey!" Kellan held up his hands, palms out. "You do *not* want to know what he spent on my medical bills in France. He's like a god in my book, for saving my bacon and all that jazz. Then again, maybe you should try to figure out what all he spent, since he deserves to be paid back."

"We can't pay him back," she said quickly, "I mean, not yet. There's no way I could charge off that kind of money to the Maddox coffers right now without attracting Grandfather's attention." Jensen Maddox could not be trusted where the imposter Kellan was concerned. They were too close. Alora eyed her brother warily, wondering if he had any idea what had been going on during his extended absence from Anchorage. "Or the attention of your imposter."

His smile disappeared. "Yeah, about that..."

She wrinkled her brow at him, walking closer to his bed to lean with both hands on the foot rail. "You're taking this really well." She didn't know what she would have done if someone had hijacked her life that way.

"I'm appalled, don't get me wrong," he made a face at her, "but no. I'm not surprised. Rhys filled me in on the flight here about the man who's stolen my life from me. I didn't know what to think of it at the time. I was still trying to make sense of the discovery I actually have a family and that he was taking me home to them." He let out an exaggerated huff and pressed his hands dramatically to his chest. "You do realize he did all this for you, right? I'm just the very lucky benefitter of the fact you lassoed the heart of someone so rich and powerful."

"That you are. Very, very lucky," she agreed tartly, not yet ready to discuss her feelings about Rhys. She wished Kellan would quit fishing for information.

"Actually, I'm pretty envious of the guy right now." He spread his hands and glanced down ruefully. "I'm here, while he's out there flying jets while wining and dining, well, *you*."

"Aww, do you want to take me to lunch, Kells?" She pushed away from his bed with a chuckle. "I can give you a raincheck, if you want."

"Sure, I'd like that. For reals." He held out his arms to her. "Come here. Gotta little something to send with you on your date."

"I don't know if it's a date," she sighed, walking around his bed to give him a hug. It was so good to have him back that she almost started weeping again.

"Oh, it's a date," he assured in a matter-of-fact tone.

"And you know this because?" she taunted as she straightened.

"I'm a guy," he announced airily. "We know stuff like..." He grinned when she picked up the pitcher of water on his nightstand and held it over his head. "Okay, so the thing is, you're hot. Anyone male who is lucky enough to wrangle a lunch with you would consider it a date."

"Nice save." She snatched up an empty cup on the side table, poured him some water, and handed it to him. "Drink up. I need you to get well as soon as possible. We have a lot of work ahead of us at DRAW Corporation, not the least of which is reinstating you as an executive."

She wasn't surprised when her words inspired a bored expression from her youngest brother. Of all their siblings, Kellan had been the least serious about his job in the past, preferring to travel the globe, attending high-end gatherings, and dating beautiful women. If there was a job title for that, he would be a pro. All her frustrations aside about his lack of commitment to the firm, however, he possessed genuine people skills that might be put to good use in the public relations arena.

He settled back in his bed and reached for the television remote. "All of a sudden, convalescing here in bed is starting to sound more appealing, now that you're dropping hints about putting me back to work."

"Get well," she snapped. "That wasn't a request."

"Aye, aye, captain." He gave her a mock salute.

She paused at the door. "Would you like me to order you some lunch before I leave?"

"Heck, no!" he exploded. "Unless they have caviar and red wine sauce on the menu—"

"They don't," she interrupted, "and you can't be

attracting that kind of attention by having stuff catered in. So whatever you were thinking of doing, don't, please. We're already doing everything we can to keep you safe until we can unseat your imposter."

"Fine!" He folded his arms, looking so much like a spoiled little boy that she smiled in sympathy.

"It won't be much longer. I promise! I have a plan."

"One that involves arresting the fake me, I hope?" He arched his brows at her. "I still don't understand why you haven't done that already."

She shook her head at him, gripping the door handle. "Maybe I'm crazy for holding off a few extra days, but I managed to get some DNA samples from him. It would be nice to know who he really is and what he really wants from us before he lawyers up. Not to mention, how he managed to so thoroughly worm his way into our grandfather's good graces. I think that's the part that makes the least sense to me about everything that went down."

"You and Grandfather never were very close," Kellan mused. He mashed a button to turn on the television but kept the sound muted.

"We have our professional differences," she conceded stiffly, not the least of which was how swiftly he'd named Kellan's imposter as interim CEO after her near-fatal car accident. The whole setup was starting to smack of collusion. She hoped she was wrong, but her grandfather and the imposter were seriously as thick as thieves.

"Uh-huh." Kellan turned up the volume on the television and started surfing channels. "Well, don't let me hold you up. I know you're in a hurry to get back to fraternizing with the enemy and all."

She leaned back inside the room to snatch up the get-well teddy bear Jacey had brought earlier and left in one of the guest chairs. Before yanking open the door, she tossed it at him.

He caught it with one hand and settled it in bed beside him. "Bye, sis!"

Rolling her eyes again, she quietly shut the door behind her. And came face-to-face with Titus Rand.

"If you're escorting me to lunch, who's going to keep an eye on the pain-in-the-rear on the other side of this door?" she demanded, hands on her hips.

He smirked down at her, touched his ear piece, and spoke softly. "You're up."

Another man in a dark suit materialized and positioned himself outside of Kellan's room.

Alora was impressed with how well-staffed Rhys's security detail was. Knowing this kind of coverage didn't come cheap, she kind of dreaded the day when she would have to settle her debts with him.

"Does Jolene Shore know you're here?" she asked cheerfully, as Titus fell in step beside her. She eyed the sling he'd been wearing for a month. Whatever injury he'd sustained to his arm was taking its precious time healing.

"Hey, I'm fine today, Alora. How are you?" he returned with a sideways glance that seemed to miss nothing.

"Oh, come on, Titus! Don't be such a stick in the mud. She's smart, pretty, and in charge!" Alora had no idea why, but she really enjoyed teasing Rhys's rigid, tight-lipped head of security.

"So are you," he shot back, "but I hear you're already taken."

Oo, way to dish it back! She felt her cheeks turn pink. "Really? Where did you hear that?"

He pointed to his ear. "Hospital walls are thin, and this device is cutting-edge."

Meaning he'd overheard her conversation with Rhys earlier...and their kiss. Her color deepened to a full blush. "So *now* you tell me."

"Sorry. It didn't come up in any of our previous conversations."

She gritted her teeth. "Is there anything you don't know about me and my family?" She knew she sounded uncharitable, considering all that he'd done for her, but she couldn't help it. She wasn't accustomed to having such a constant set of eyes and ears on her every move. Sure, she'd employed bodyguards in the past, but usually only to escort her to major public gatherings.

They reached her Land Rover in the parking

garage. "Would you like me to drive or lead the caravan?"

She eyed his sling again. "Why? Did you drive your motorcycle again?"

He gave an off-hand shrug. "It's my only ride."

Figuring he'd be more comfortable inside her vehicle in a leather captain's chair, she relented. "Fine. You can drive." She dug out her key fob, mashed a button to unlock the doors, and started the engine remotely.

He walked her around to the passenger side and held open her door.

"Thanks." She climbed in and buckled her seatbelt.

He drove in silence through the winding streets of the city without turning on any main highways. Alora watched as he glanced repeatedly through the side mirrors as well as the rearview mirror. He circled one of the ritzy residential avenues twice, before pulling into a secluded side street.

"Are we being followed?" she asked sharply, surprised to discover they were in her neighborhood. It was an older, well-established section of town, punctuated by homes on hills with magnificent views.

"No, I made sure of it." He turned into one of the many private driveways. This one was sheltered by tall, stately trees, and there was a no-trespassing sign at the mailbox. He drove around a curve and braked at an ornate iron gate. Rolling down the window, he leaned out and typed a code into the keypad. The gate slowly swung open.

Titus drove up a winding hill with stunning, drop-off views just beyond a stone knee wall. They approached an enormous structure built cleverly into the hillside. For a moment, Alora wondered if they'd arrived at some sort of private resort.

Several of the exterior walls were made of solid glass, others boasted rustic cherry wood panels, and there were too many balconies and outsets to count at first glance. One extended deck boasted an infinity pool that likely made the swimmer feel like they could paddle straight into the horizon, itself. A large, circular dome on the third story boasted a helicopter pad with a sleek white bird resting atop it.

"Is this his home?" Her heartbeat increased, because that would essentially make her and Rhys neighbors. How had she not known this?

"It is." Titus braked in the middle of a wide circle drive. He swiftly turned off the engine and jogged around to her side of the vehicle to open her door.

Alora shaded a hand over her eyes. "I can see the roofline of my home from here." It was a fifty-year-old, Tudor-style mansion set on a smaller hill. She'd had it entirely remodeled during the past few years. It was uncanny to realize that Rhys had been her neighbor all this time. During the winter months, when the trees were bare, he'd have a much clearer view of her home.

Apparently, there were a great many things she didn't know about the man she'd agreed to have lunch with.

CHAPTER 6: LUNCH DATE

RHYS

R hys swung open the door of his sunroom, monumentally grateful that Alora had kept her word to meet him for lunch. A part of him had feared she wouldn't — not that he anticipated her deliberately standing him up, per se, so much as getting called back into work to put out a fire.

"You came." He held out a hand to her and was thrilled when she accepted it.

"I said I would."

He nodded at Titus over her head and held his gaze for a moment to silently ask if he had any news about the fake Kellan's identity.

Titus gave a slight shake of his head, then held up his phone and pointed to the screen to indicate he'd send Rhys a message when he heard back about the DNA tests.

Rhys nodded again, and Titus took off in the

direction of the guest house. It was on the other side of his ten-bay garage, giving his occasional visitors maximum privacy while they enjoyed his rim lot views.

He greatly appreciated the fact that Titus had driven Alora and that she'd let him. It was progress in their highly non-conventional relationship. He was fairly certain not many men had to go to the lengths he'd gone to protect the women they love. By now, Alora was well aware of the massive security detail he had surrounding her, but she had yet to voice a complaint.

"Both Titus and Kellan know about us," she announced without preamble, as he led her through the sunroom to his front veranda. It was where his personal chef would be serving their lunch.

"Yes. I told them."

Her fingers briefly tightened on his. "Who else knows?"

"Luca." His oldest brother had been the first to find out. They'd always been close and rarely kept secrets from each other. It was one of the reasons they worked so well together at the helm of Genesis & Sons. They always communicated and always had each other's backs.

"What about Jacey?"

He shook his head. "Luca doesn't care to keep secrets from his wife, but he figures it's your place to tell your sister when you're ready."

"Thank you," she said softly.

He opened the wide, sliding glass door to the veranda and heard her catch her breath.

"Rhys! It's gorgeous out here." She let go of his hand and stepped into the sunshine, smoothing her hair back as the breezes played through it.

Chef Heston had outdone himself, setting up a small, round table for two. It boasted a white linen tablecloth and a tumble of wildflowers and fruit for a centerpiece. A pair of chilled flutes sparkled with one of Heston's hand-mixed flavored waters.

"I've always thought so." Having a home with spectacular views like this pleased him more than all the works of art he owned in his private gallery. "God's own artwork," he mused. He loved how the hills and ridges changed with the lighting throughout the day, the temperament of the weather, and the colors unique to each season.

"I couldn't have said it better." She gave up smoothing her hair and, instead, pulled out a few pins to let it tumble around her shoulders.

It was his turn to catch his breath. "The views are particularly stunning today," he said quietly. Her hair caught the sun and shone like fire against the fabric of her blue-gray suit.

"Thank you." She blushed and tucked a lock behind one ear. "What's on the menu?"

"Coho salmon, fresh herb risotto, and a strawberry-pineapple gazpacho."

"That sounds amazing." She pressed a hand to her flat midsection. "I haven't had much of an appetite lately, but suddenly I'm starving."

He was glad to hear it. She'd always been a willowy kind of slender, but she was especially thin these days. Too thin. He considered himself to be a pretty non-critical guy when it came to a woman's unique size and shape; however, even he could tell her clothing was too loose. Her hospital stay had taken its toll on her. He wished he was in the position to have his chef take over her meal preparation.

Chef Heston Iacuzzi was, quite simply, the best when it came to stirring up feasts in the kitchen. He didn't simply stir up beautiful, award-winning displays, although he was more than capable of doing so when Rhys entertained larger groups. Most days, Heston spent his time meticulously designing individualized meal plans for each member of Rhys's household and served up the perfect entrees for their dietary needs. Rhys considered the man worth every penny of the six-figure salary he paid him.

Soft music filtered through Rhys's built-in, surround-sound system. He was playing the live recording of a stringed ensemble he'd had the pleasure of enjoying at a symphony hall in Venice.

Alora consumed more than he expected of the Coho Salmon but not as much as he hoped. She fiddled with her fork over the gazpacho, and he could tell she was filling up.

"How do you find time for things like this?" she asked suddenly, turning her inquisitive gaze to his. Against the backdrop of the green foliage on his veranda, her eyes appeared more green than blue. "Not just for this extraordinary lunch, but for all you've done for me and my family in recent days," she added in a sweetly wistful tone. "I know first-hand how busy a schedule most executives have to keep. It couldn't have been easy for you to do every-thing you've done."

"Like every executive worth the powder to blow them up, I make time for what's important," he returned without hesitation. "You're important to me, Alora."

Her eyelashes fluttered against her cheeks, and she caught her lower lip between her teeth.

Before she could respond, however, Chef Heston silently appeared to swap out their near-empty, berry-flavored sparkling water for refills in frosted wine glasses. His tousled blonde hair was in its usual disarray, though his chef's coat was pristine white and impeccably pressed.

Rhys nodded his appreciation. For some reason, the sight of the man generally amused him. Heston was an interesting character, a bit on the tempera-mental side, though he possessed a heart of gold beneath his moody veneer. He also tended to work best when his cooking was showered with compliments.

His chef nodded back. "Was everything to your satisfaction, ma'am?" He worriedly eyed Alora's half-eaten meal.

"It was divine," she assured with a grateful smile. "Don't mind me. I'm still working up an appetite after an extended convalescence."

The concern lines deepened at the corners of his eyes. "Is there anything else I can get you?" he inquired anxiously.

"The sparkling water is more than enough, thank you." She inclined her head graciously as she raised her crystal flute to take a sip. "This is amazing, by the way. I don't recognize the brand."

"I mixed it myself."

"No wonder it's so good."

Chef Heston bowed to her, visibly preening, and his hazel eyes glowed as he took his leave of them.

"Good gracious, Rhys! Lunch was superb," Alora declared after he left. "I don't even know how to begin thanking you for all you've done. For all you're still doing for me." She set down her crystal glass.

"I'm not looking for thanks." He reached across the table for her hand.

She stared at their joined fingers, a faint smile playing across her lips. "I know you aren't, but—"

"I'm playing a longer game, Alora, but I think you've probably figured that out by now." He wanted it all — her loyalty, her trust, and her heart.

"Why me?" she asked quietly. "I honestly thought you despised me, Rhys."

He groaned inwardly, knowing she was referring to that one unfortunate cotillion they'd attended together years ago. "I never despised you." He'd hated the way the other guys had kept cutting in while he was trying to dance with her. Unfortunately, he'd taken his frustration out on her by saying some pretty inexcusable things that he'd regretted ever since.

She made an amused sound, though she thankfully didn't withdraw her hand from his. "I believe the words you called me that fateful evening were shallow and manipulative."

This time Rhys didn't bother suppressing his groan. "I was young and stupid," he confessed in a contrite tone. "And jealous, if you must know."

"Of whom?" She wrinkled her nose at him, still smiling. "You're a forbidden Calcagni, and I'm a hated Maddox. We were supposed to be avoiding each other like poison."

"I was envious of every guy you danced with that evening who wasn't me," he admitted, toying with her fingers. "I resented the fact that..." He stopped, knowing there was no point in rehashing the past.

But she wasn't ready to let it go. "You accused me of using men, but not being able to see them for who they really are."

"It was a hateful thing to say. I was wrong."

"No, you were right."

His gaze locked on hers, surprised at the vehemence in her voice.

Her eyes were stricken. "I wasn't raised to see people for who they are or to be compassionate. I was raised to compete." Her voice turned bitter. "To be the best at everything I did, no matter the cost. I competed with everyone, including my own siblings. Heck! Our family encouraged it." She sighed. "They were forever pitting us against each other. It's a wonder any of us are still on speaking terms."

He made a scoffing sound. "I hear what you're saying, but I think you're being a little hard on yourself. The truth is, you are good at what you do. Very good. Your siblings respect you for it and look to you for leadership." He cradled her hand between his. "They were lost without you, while you were in the hospital. Completely shattered at the thought of losing you for good." He drew a deep breath. "We all were."

Her eyes misted. "I appreciate your kind words, but the truth is, my siblings and I were barely on speaking terms before the accident. Jacey took off as soon as she could, just to get away from it all. Greyson had pretty much turned into a recluse, hiding out in his techno labs 24/7, and Kellan..." She shook her head regretfully. "How long was he gone before we even realized he was missing?"

"Hey, now," Rhys chided softly, "he had a look-alike standing in for him. That sort of blurred the lines a little, don't you think?"

"I should have known," she snapped, but he knew her anger was directed at herself more than him. "I'm his sister. Then there's Bailey, the sweetest spirit among us, who was always trying to keep the peace and nearly got drummed out of the family business for her troubles. My car accident served as my wake up call. Things can't continue as they are, Rhys. I have to do better. DRAW Corporation has to do better."

"You *are* doing better," he assured. "You've been in office for how long? A month? And the first thing you did was honor your marketing contract with Titan Industries." He knew this, because the news of her decision had taken the headlines by storm. It was a daring and risky move, since DRAW's ten-year marketing contract with Titan had been put in place by Kellan's imposter for the precise purpose of outsourcing Bailey's position as the Vice President of Marketing at DRAW — in other words, to render her irrelevant and obsolete. With Luca's assistance, however, Don had turned the tables on Kellan, bought out Titan Industries, and handed the reins of the business over to his new bride, essentially restoring everything that had been wrongfully taken from her.

"Thank you." Alora looked tired. "I'm trying,

Rhys. Unfortunately, I have a lot to make up for, things that aren't going to be fixed overnight."

"So pace yourself," he advised, admiring the perfect taper of her nails and their bright pink lacquer. She wore a lot of all-business gray, black, navy, and browns; but she tended to spice up her outfits with elegant shoes and bright pops of nail color. He'd always adored that about her, that small streak of adventure, that hint at something special — well beyond the ordinary — just like the woman inside. "Running a company is a marathon, not a sprint."

"Normally, I would agree with that statement." She bowed her head over their hands. "But not every new CEO has a family member gunning for their job and, quite frankly, their life."

"No," he agreed. Most new CEOs didn't have someone gunning for the jobs and wellbeing of the rest of their siblings, either. "I say this calls for a special strategy, one that begins and ends with taking care of yourself, Alora." He ducked his head to look her in the eye and had to wait until she glanced up again.

"Rhys, I can't sleep more, if that's what you're implying. I don't have the time. I shouldn't even be here right now, enjoying this amazing lunch with your incredible self."

"Thank you for the compliment." He smiled tenderly at her. "So, if you can't reduce your work hours, then you need to stay as rested and as fit as possible while on the move, don't you agree? Giving your body the maximum opportunity to heal, even while you stay busy."

She gave a humorless chuckle, cocking her heart-shaped face at him. "Unless you have a bottle of pixie dust lying around, Mr. Calcagni..."

He waggled his brows at her, adoring the light sprinkling of freckles across her nose and wanting to kiss each one. "Maybe I do, love."

She went still at the endearment, her eyes shyly scanning his face.

He hadn't meant to call her that. It had simply slipped out, as naturally as he breathed. It was how he thought of her.

"I'm listening," she declared, a bit breathlessly.

"Okay, maybe not a bottle of pixie dust, but better, I think. She's a masseuse named Friday."

Alora's smile widened. "Is that her real name?"

"I doubt it; but I don't know and don't care every time she's working the kinks from my neck and shoulders." He waggled his brows at her again. "Want to give her magical hands a spin?"

"Well, how can I say no to that?" She reached out to touch the flower petals in the centerpiece. "If you give me her contact information, I'll give her a call soon."

"Or you can give her a few minutes of your time before Titus drives you to the office." Rhys enjoyed the surprised look that flitted across Alora's face, then the incredulity. "You won't regret the small delay. I guarantee it," he added slyly.

Alora's expression settled into stunned lines. "You have a masseuse on your staff, too?"

"More like on speed dial. Come on!" He lightly tugged on her hand. "I can lend you a robe." He stood and pulled her to her feet.

"You planned this!" She bit her lower lip to muffle a surprised laugh.

"Guilty as charged."

"Rhys, I don't know what to say." She faced him, shaking her head and smiling wistfully.

"Come on. You know you want to," he taunted.

"My better judgment says no, but my aching neck is begging me to change my mind," she bemoaned.

His gaze dropped to her neck, which had only recently come out of its cervical collar. "It's alright. I've already briefed Friday on your recent injuries. I assure you she's very well trained in rehabilitation therapies."

Alora tapped her lips with one finger, flashing her brightly painted nail at him. "I don't know if I possess the willpower to say no to such a kind and thoughtful offer."

"Then don't." He was thrilled by her capitulation, knowing she could desperately use the kind of services Friday offered. "You're a CEO known for your wise decisions." He winked at her and led her inside to the sunroom, which was essentially a wall of windows.

Friday already had her white leather massage table set up. Her roller cart of supplies was resting next to it, complete with her array of oils, creams, and — joy of joys — her portable towel warmer. She glanced up when they walked into the room and immediately hopped off her silver stool. She was a tall, wiry tarantula of a woman in a white smock and white Birkenstock sandals. Her black hair was trimmed short, and her expressive mouth stretched into a wide, welcoming smile.

"Miss Maddox?" Friday bobbed her head. "I'm so glad you decided to try out my services. You won't regret it." Her swift glance took in the fact that Alora's hand was still entwined with Rhys's.

"So I've heard from one rave reviewer." Alora smiled up at him as she slid her hand from his.

He wondered if she even noticed that Friday had noticed they were holding hands. It didn't matter, at any rate. Friday understood his need for complete confidentiality. Besides, it was carefully spelled out in their contract.

Ignoring his intense longing to bend his head over Alora's and say goodbye with a kiss, he quietly backed from the room to give her and Friday their privacy.

Alora rejoined him on the veranda approximately forty-five minutes later.

He watched her loose-limbed approach from where he was lounging against the railing. She was back in her suit, her makeup refreshed, and her hair returned to its lovely up-do. *That's it. Come to me, love.* He reached for her hand once she was standing in front of him. "How do you feel?"

"Like a new person," she confessed softly. "Thank you. For everything. I guess you've heard me say that so much lately, I'm starting to sound like a broken record."

"How's the neck?" He frowned down at her delicate throat.

"Much better, thanks to Friday," she admitted. "It was hurting all morning, but not any longer."

"I suspected as much." He grimaced.

"Of course you did." Alora took a step closer, treating him to an intoxicating whiff of her flowery scent. "You seem to be really skilled at reading me."

"It's a skill I've been working on for years."

"I wish things could be different for us right now," she exclaimed with a sad look. "If we were a normal couple, I would thank you with a kiss, and we would be delightfully distracted for another half hour that we can't afford in either of our busy schedules."

Rhys's heart pounded from her nearness, wanting more than anything to take her words for the invitation they were. However, he'd promised himself he would take things slow with her. That he would romance her in the classy way she deserved, not skipping any steps along the way.

"It's okay. I've got my goal in sight, and I'm a patient man." He gazed deeply into her eyes. "I'm not going anywhere, Alora."

"Me neither, Rhys." She reached up to touch his cheek, and he forgot all his good intentions to go slow.

His mouth descended toward hers; but, before their lips could touch, both their phones sounded off with incoming messages. Hers trilled out a ring, and his vibrated in his pocket.

"I guess I lied about going anywhere," she teased ruefully. "Work calls."

While Rhys dug out his phone, Alora crossed the veranda to retrieve hers from her purse, which was resting beside her chair. He allowed himself to enjoy the sight of her feet and ankles encased in strappy, bright pink stilettos.

"Alora Maddox speaking." Her tone was crisp and all-business again.

Man! He admired her unshakable poise and her ability to pull on a professional face at a moment's notice.

The message on his phone was from Titus Rand. The DNA tests for the imposter had been run. Rhys couldn't have been more floored by their results.

He watched Alora's contented expression tense. "I'm on my way." She clicked off the connection, shaking her head. "Well, thank you again for this amazing escape from the real world." She slid the strap of her handbag over her shoulder and tucked her phone back inside it. "That was my assistant, informing me of an unscheduled board meeting that totally smacks of Kellan's imposter's interference. Apparently, I'm being called before them to defend my position of honoring our contract with Titan Industries."

"Which you will do in spades," he said firmly. "You made the right decision for all the right reasons. Go sell it to them, love."

"Thank you, Rhys." Her expression softened. "You always seem to know what I need to hear."

Points for the boyfriend. At least, he hoped that's what she considered him to be, at this point.

"What kind of news did you receive?" She scanned his face, and her smile slipped.

"Not what I was expecting." His jaw tightened as he waved his phone at her. "The DNA results came back."

Alora pressed a hand to her chest and drew a shallow breath. "And?"

"The imposter is biologically related to Kellan."

"Please, no!" she breathed, paling a few degrees.

"The lab technician thinks we're looking at identical twins."

CHAPTER 7: BOARD GAMES

ALORA

Alora glided back to the table to snatch up her flute of sparkling water. "Say a prayer for me, Rhys. This is going to be the most difficult meeting I've ever attended." One in which she would be forced to pretend everything was normal, while sitting across the table from a man who wanted her dead. A man who, most unfortunately, might also be the biological brother of someone she loved.

"You can't just walk into that board meeting like nothing has changed," Rhys declared hoarsely. "He's a felon, guilty of criminal impersonation in the first degree."

"Which we can't prove," she countered, closing her eyes to think. "At least not yet. Right now, all we can prove is criminal impersonation in the second degree, which is nothing more than a misdemeanor. Although he has spent some of Kellan's money and enjoyed benefits that do not legally belong to him, he has mostly allowed our grandfather to pick up the tab for his expenses. In court, that could be construed as a gift. Plus, Kellan's investment portfolios have grown significantly during the past few months, which might make it tricky to prove reckless damage to his financial reputation."

"It's too dangerous," Rhys protested. "Please, Alora, it's time to call the police." He followed her to the table, his expression grim.

"Not yet." She shook her head, looking pale and drawn. "You just told me that Kellan has a twin. As much as I don't like the guy, that makes him family." She took another sip of her water. "At the very least, Kellan deserves to know he has a twin before we have him arrested. This feels like something my other siblings would want to weigh in on, too."

Good heavens! They'd only recently discovered they were adopted — all five Maddox children — and now to learn that one of them had a twin who had failed to be adopted. An identical twin, no less! It was stretching the boundaries of everything Alora knew to be true about her parents. Sure, they were unemotional and not overly affectionate, but how could they be so cruel and unfeeling as to separate twins? Her mind raced at the knowledge that each of her siblings had been adopted at a very young age, which meant the twins had been separated at birth or shortly afterward. Did her parents even know about Kellan's twin? Maybe someone else had separated the brothers at birth, unbeknownst to them.

Clearly, however, Kellan's twin had found out. Instead of making an effort to meet his twin, however, he'd chosen to hijack his identity. Why?

"He tried to kill you, Alora!" Rhys reminded in a low, angry voice.

"We don't know that for sure," she reminded weakly. "We all assumed that, because he's gone to such extremes to oust us from our positions at DRAW; but what if he had nothing to do with my car accident? What if it truly was an accident?"

"It was a hit-and-run," he declared tersely. "With the extent of the injuries you sustained, it is likely to be ruled a felony."

"I agree, but that still doesn't prove Kellan's twin did it."

Rhys stepped closer to cup her face in his hands. "Listen to me, Alora. If there is any chance Kellan's twin could be dangerous, it's not a risk I'm willing to take with your safety. I almost lost you once." His voice grew hoarse. "You can't ask this of me."

"I understand, and I appreciate your concern. Truly." The tender anxiousness in his expression was making her knees weak.

"Concern!" he scoffed in a tight voice. "More like out of my mind with worry."

"I'm so sorry." She closed her eyes to momentarily block out his frantic expression. She couldn't think clearly when he was looking at her like that. "I hear what you're saying, and I know you're right; but my heart isn't in it. It's too soon to stop our investigation and call the police. We need to first dig deeper and find out more. We need to be very sure Kellan's twin is guilty before we help put him behind bars." Her eyelids flew open. "I also need you to tell me what I can do to give you some peace of mind while I attend my board meeting, Rhys." She blinked as a thought struck her. "I could take Titus with me."

"And Major, my driver." Rhys bent his head to tip his forehead against hers. "He's my personal bodyguard. I trust him implicitly."

"Who will protect you, then?"

"Just do it, please." He raised his head to brush his lips against her hairline. "Titus says he thinks he can call in a favor from an FBI friend to help determine who the imposter really is. Name, vocation, that sort of thing."

"Thank you so much." Alora smiled in amazement. His resources were truly limitless. "Wow! You and I really are going to have to sit down soon and settle my debts. I know you keep saying you don't want my money, Rhys, but sheesh! You have to allow me to contribute something."

"Fine!" he growled. "We'll work something out soon." His lips twitched. "Over dinner."

"What? You're wrangling another date out of this?" she teased.

"Yes. You caught me. I'm shameless." He bent to kiss her forehead again. "I need you to agree to one more thing."

"Sure. What is it?" She was relieved that her agreement to take a pair of his bodyguards to her board meeting seemed to calm him down.

"I need you to sit with a sketch artist and tell them everything you can remember about the truck that hit you." So far, no big black trucks with collision damage had surfaced in town, despite an ongoing search by the local police. "In the absence of a license number, we need to try to identify make and model."

"I'll do it," she promised. "In the meantime, I'll send an update to my siblings about the latest developments. We were already planning to reconvene this evening at the hospital. Can I count on you to be there?"

"You can." He claimed her mouth. "You can always count on me, love," he swore fiercely between kisses.

"I don't deserve you," she sighed when he finally raised his head.

"Whatever." He ran his thumb over her lower lip. "Alright, love. Go face the lions. I'll see you in a few hours."

Alora knew she should be preparing her defense; but during the short drive to DRAW Corporation, all she could do was think about Rhys and his kisses.

Major drove them, and Titus sat next to him in the passenger seat. When they turned on to the street where her firm was located, he twisted around in his seat to smirk at her. "Might want to freshen up your lipstick, princess. Otherwise, someone besides me might guess what you and my boss have really been up to."

"Guess?" she inquired sarcastically, while diving for her tube of lipstick in her purse. "Last time I checked, the line of business you happen to be in was called eavesdropping."

"Not this time," he informed her cheerfully. "You just have that glow about you, of a woman who's been thoroughly kissed."

"Well, put on a pair of sunglasses," she retorted, holding up her compact mirror to apply a new layer of lipstick.

"Thank you. I will." He produced a pair of black shades with silver rims and put them on. It made him look like such a stereotypical bodyguard that she had to smother a chuckle, not wanting to give him the satisfaction of knowing he amused her with his antics.

"You know, if security ends up not being your thing, you can always head to Hollywood. I hear they're looking for extras on the set of Mall Cop 3."

"Good idea. I love that show." He pushed his shades higher up his nose with one finger.

She found herself at serious risk of starting to like

the guy. He was growing on her, now that he was starting to unwind a bit in her presence.

"Hey, how's the bulging bicep up there?" she inquired, reaching for her briefcase. "I meant to ask you earlier." She needed to review her notes on the Pezel account before returning the call to their acquisitions manager this afternoon. They were asking for an exclusive contract to manufacture a new line of dog sleds being designed by another DRAW client.

"It's responding to therapy." His tone was cautious as he shot her a wary glance over his shoulder.

"Glad to hear it. When's your next appointment?" She hastily scanned her notes.

"That's need-to-know. Why do you ask?"

"So I can inform Nurse Shore the next time you plan to show up at the hospital," she breezed. "See? I clearly need to know." She closed the client file, confident that she was ready. As for her showdown with the board, she intended to adopt a tone of gracious transparency and simply speak from her heart. Bailey was one of theirs, even though her business card bore a different logo these days.

Titus leaned across the console to speak in a loud whisper to Major. "If she asks, you're a chicken farmer from Peru."

"I am?" Major glanced at Alora through the rearview mirror and cleared his throat, looking uncomfortable.

"Yep. Already married with six kids."

"Wow, I've been busy," Major chuckled.

"And you'll stay busy, bro." Titus clapped him on the shoulder. "No time for anything but working hard and saving for all that college tuition."

"I'm disappointed," Alora said in a tone of fake mourning. "I was actually considering giving up on Titus and setting you up, instead, on a blind date with Nurse Shore."

It was nearly imperceptible, but Alora was very perceptive when it came to reading body language. And unless she had something stuck in her eye, Titus twitched at her suggestion.

"Aha! You scowled." She wagged her finger at him. "That means you don't like the idea of Jolene Shore dating anyone else."

"I'm always scowling." He angled his head at their driver. "Isn't that right, Major?"

"Yep. Permanent scowl." Major nodded. "A mad dog snarl that scares children and makes small puppies run."

"Good." Alora closed her briefcase. "Now look tough, boys, because we have some real demons to face this afternoon."

"Oh, goody!" Major braked at the front entrance of the gorgeous white and chrome high-rise that housed DRAW's corporate headquarters. He rubbed his hands together. "It'll be great practice for when I take my large brood trick-or-treating in a few months." He bent his head closer to Titus's. "A large family is a brood, right? Not a herd? Or a litter?"

Titus shrugged. "Come to think of it, chickens also run in broods, though I've never seen them trick-or-treating." He opened his door and swung his large body out. "Wouldn't mind seeing it, though, now that you mention it."

Major waved both his hands to shoo him out of the vehicle. "Tough crowd. That's it; I'm heading back to Peru, where I'm appreciated."

"After my meeting, please," Alora nodded her thanks to Titus for opening her door, "because I'm considering firing him." She stuck a thumb in Titus's direction.

Titus shrugged at Major. "I could always join you in Peru."

Major shook his head and rolled his window down to converse with the valet. He handed over Alora's key fob, then joined them on the sidewalk. The three of them passed through the front rotating glass door.

"Afternoon, Miss Maddox!" A guard waved her past the security checkpoint without scanning her, though he stopped Titus and Major. He made them empty their pockets, flash their weapons, and pass through his metal detector.

"Was that really necessary?" Titus grumbled as he buttoned his shirt back over the holster he had strapped to his chest. He glanced up to take in the three-story lobby with its modern, square wire fixtures. They were suspended from the ceiling, dripping with teardrop shaped bulbs. Opposite the front wall of glass, there was an enormous clock made of all silver slash marks with no numbers displayed. In the center of the white tiled room was a set of red leather sofas with minimal-istic square lines, arranged into a U-shaped lounge area. A water feature cascaded down the east wall.

"Nope. Putting you through that wasn't the least bit necessary." She chuckled as she led them past the receptionist's booth on the west side of the room, through a door marked *Authorized Personnel Only.* "I was just curious about how much heat you were packing."

Titus scowled at her. "Can I fire myself and go home, already?"

"To Peru?"

He shook his head in disgust at her.

"Don't bother," she retorted gayly. "Rhys would just rehire you."

Once inside the elevator, all the gaiety in her dried up. She could feel the start of a headache coming on. She reached up to rub her right temple as the number over the door flashed their progress up to the top floor.

"You're going to do fine in there," Titus noted quietly.

"I'm not nervous," she protested, gripping the handle of her briefcase more tightly.

"So you're *not* deflecting your anxiety by roasting all the poor souls in your employ?" He followed her line of vision to watch the flashing number over the door. "My mistake."

"Apology accepted," she shot back. "I'm perfectly calm." She closed her eyes momentarily and drew a deep breath. The elevator doors rolled open, and she swayed on her feet for a second.

"You've got this, Alora Maddox," Titus rumbled low in her ear, nudging her elbow with his good arm.

ALORA MADE a quick detour to her top-floor office to drop off her briefcase, before heading down the hall to the board room. Her family was already assembled at the long, mahogany table when she swept into the room.

She was surprised to note that her parents were present. Neither Nora nor Pierce Maddox had bothered to notify her of their return from overseas. Jensen Maddox was presiding at the head of the table. Though he was no longer the CEO of DRAW, he'd not yet given up the spot and likely never would. Greyson was seated to his left, with his delightfully disheveled hair. His endearing bowtie was fire engine red. He'd paired it with a pinstripe charcoal suit and gray dress shirt. Kellan's imposter was seated immediately to her grandfather's right, all swanky in yet another new-looking suit.

Alora tried not to stare too long at him, though she was careful to briefly meet his eye and nod like she did to the others. It was hard, though. *You're my brother's identical twin, huh?* It was mind boggling to the extreme. "Welcome back from wherever you've been, Kells," she trilled as she breezed past him. "Haven't seen much of you the last few days." It was the third time in the past month he'd mysteriously disappeared for a full twenty-four hours.

His shoulders stiffened. "I've been working," he informed her coolly. "And you? I came looking for you an hour ago, but your assistant said you were gone all morning."

"I was in meetings, sweetie," she cooed. "You know how it is, considering your recent stint as our interim CEO." She bent to air-kiss her mother's cheek as she glided past her.

Nora Maddox was tapping her blood-red nails on the table. "Hired yourself some new muscle, daughter?" she asked in a low voice.

"Oh, right." Alora pasted on a smile as she took her place behind the clear, glass podium at the front of the room. She reached for the remote control and flipped on the overhead projector. While it was warming up, she nodded at her pair of bodyguards, who'd positioned themselves against the wall on either side of the conference table. "Good afternoon, everyone. Since Mother asked, I'd like to start by introducing my two newest bodyguards, Major and Titus. Because of recent events, I felt it would be wise to take extra precautions."

Greyson nodded vehemently, and her father looked unexpectedly approving.

Her mother, however, looked suspicious. "So long as you're not canoodling with them like Bailey." She gave a fake shudder and smoothed a hand over her shoulder-length, platinum blonde hair.

"Well, no worry with Major in that regard. He's from Peru," she announced gayly. "A chicken farmer with a wife and six children. He's up here in the great state of Alaska, pulling security to save for their college tuition. As for Titus," she angled her head at him, "he's dating a nurse at the Gjoa Haven Medical Center. Then again, you didn't call me into this special meeting of the board to discuss the love lives of my bodyguards, did you? On the contrary..." She mashed a button on her remote control, and a life-sized portrait of Bailey Maddox Kappelman popped onto the screen. "You asked me to share some insight into my decision to honor our exclusive marketing contract with Titan Industries."

She paused to shoot a beaming smile in Kellan's direction. "As you well know, this contract was negotiated and put into place by our very own Kellan Maddox while I was in the hospital. I want to congratulate him on his excellent research into one of the top marketing firms in the world. I highly approve his choice." She rattled off the sales and revenue figures of the company, along with the names of some of their biggest contracts. "They have a proven track record that will benefit our company in the coming days, months, and years."

"Alora," her mother sighed, "no one is questioning Kellan's good judgment here. We are questioning yours, or rather your wisdom in honoring the contract now that the company is under new ownership."

"Under the ownership of one of our own," Alora pointed out. "While Bailey served as the Vice President of Marketing at DRAW Corporation, she increased revenue across the board on website advertising, social media monetizing, and other income streams. Her marketing project designs are cutting edge, visionary, and effective in terms of profitability. It is my firm belief, as a DRAW insider, that she understands our mission like no one else and is best poised to oversee this leg of our business."

"You assigned the next marketing campaign of our biggest client to Titan." Greyson folded his arms and fixed her with what he probably thought was a hard stare. It nearly made her chuckle. "I'd like to know why."

"Like I said, Bailey is the best talent we have in our repertoire. Our biggest client deserves the best marketing expertise we can offer. Do you have any better ideas than delivering the services of the one and only Bailey Maddox Kappelman?" Alora had not put Greyson up to questioning her like this, but she liked his line of questioning. She knew her answers would only make Bailey shine all that brighter.

Nora Maddox's bright red painted lips tightened into a flat line. She knew Alora was right, but she never liked to admit when she was wrong. "What if you're wrong about her new priorities? Then what?"

"Oh, come on!" Alora threw up her hands. "It's Bailey we're talking about here. Your daughter. My sister." She rolled her eyes. "I think everyone here would agree she's as close to a saint as any Maddox is ever going to be." She purposefully hammered home the point that Bailey was still a Maddox, knowing that was the biggest sticking point with her audience.

Her words garnered a few chuckles and knowing nods.

"However, if you're truly concerned about her ability to continue providing us the same quality of marketing expertise she's always provided us, despite the full backing and resources of a Fortune 500 company at her disposal, I'm willing to put her contract on a probationary period. Either Titan will re-prove its worth to us and the rest of the world, or we'll go back to the drawing board." She had no doubt Bailey would deliver.

"Guess that works for me." Greyson waved two fingers in the air.

Her mother nodded grudgingly. "I'm still not thrilled about Bailey leaving the company, but I guess testing out one contract with her won't hurt. At least we know what we're getting ourselves into in our dealings with her."

"Nor I," her father intoned. He nearly always shadowed his wife's decisions. Alora had no doubt his mind was already on his next golf outing.

Jensen Maddox held Alora's gaze for a few moments longer, his heavily lined face twisted into an inscrutable expression. Then he nodded. That signified the challenge was over. For now.

Kellan didn't vote. With a vengeful glance in her direction, he scooped up a file folder from the table in front of him and pushed back his chair. As he headed for the door, Alora followed him.

"Hold up there, Kellan. We need to talk."

He slowly pivoted on the heels of his wine-colored wingtips, casting an uncertain glance in Jensen Maddox's direction. Her grandfather paused in his exodus, as if trying to decide if he should remain in the room.

He knows! The discovery that her grandfather knew Kellan wasn't the real Kellan stunned Alora more than anything else in the last twenty-four hours. She covered her choking horror with a cough.

"I haven't yet taken the time to properly thank

you for everything you did while I was in my coma," she said, hating that she sounded a trifle winded.

Kellan's twin's expression turned sour. "I can tell, seeing as you've spent the past month undoing everything I put into place." He shot a bitter glance at Titus and Major, who'd stepped closer during the exchange.

She was so taken aback by the viciousness of his response, that she was momentarily at a loss for how to respond. It was one thing to disagree with someone professionally; it was another thing entirely for that person to openly attack her inside the walls of her own company.

Her grandfather laid a gentle hand on the imposter Kellan's shoulder. "How about you head on over to my office? I'll meet you there in two snaps, and we can head out for coffee."

After one last angry glance at Alora, the fake Kellan smoothed a hand down the front of his designer herringbone suit, and left the room, still shaking his head.

"Coffee?" Alora was too incensed to mince words with her grandfather. She folded her arms and prepared to engage in a verbal duel. "That's your response to what just happened? Coffee?"

To her surprise, her grandfather ran a hand tiredly over his face, then waved at the table they'd just vacated. "Do you mind sitting? I have something to tell you."

She held up a hand and backed toward the table. "I'm all ears." She deliberately took the chair at the head of it and fixed a glare on him. Titus took his position behind her seat, while Major moved to stand by the door.

Her grandfather stood next to the table, completely ignoring her bodyguards as if they didn't exist, for an extended moment before taking the seat to her right. "You look good there, Alora. I always knew you would."

Her lips parted. It was the last thing she expected him to say, considering how reluctant he'd been to hand over the corporate reins to her in recent months.

He sank heavily into his chair and pressed his hands on the table in front of him. "It's obvious to me that you've figured out Kellan isn't exactly himself these days."

Because he's not Kellan, you fool! A strangled sound of incredulity escaped her as she realized how wrong she'd been in her first assumption. Her grandfather had no idea they were dealing with an imposter.

Jensen Maddox lowered his voice and dipped his head closer to hers. "Your parents are the only other ones who know about this, but Kellan was in a boating accident during his last trip overseas. He suffered a traumatic head injury that has resulted in some — let's just say — unfortunate symptoms."

"Such as?" Alora's voice shook. This was worse than she imagined. It meant Kellan's twin knew, possibly firsthand, about Kellan's accident and had capitalized on it in the most diabolical way. Her mind raced over the possibilities. Had he caused the accident, himself? Did he believe the real Kellan to be dead? Otherwise, he had to know his current game would be short-lived. What was his ultimate goal? Draining Kellan's assets and skipping town?

Her grandfather cast her a look of concern and covered her hands with his. "He may never be the same, Alora." He ducked his head and sniffed damply. "This new version of Kellan may be what we're left with for good." He appeared to be struggling to maintain his composure. "I'm trying to get him the help he needs, but you know Kellan. Always treating life like it's one big party. So far, I haven't succeeded in getting him to keep many of his doctor's appointments."

Alora shook her head, struggling to find her voice. "Keep trying," she finally managed to choke out. Her brain wrestled with a snarl of unanswered questions.

"I will." Her grandfather released her hands to dash the backs of his over his eyes. He regarded her wearily, looking suddenly old. "About that coffee, hon."

"Go!" She waved at him, dangerously close to

breaking down right there in the boardroom. "I'll, ah...catch up with you soon."

He nodded, his expression crumpling as he surveyed her. "At least I got one of you back."

His uncharacteristic show of emotion made the tears Alora was trying to hold back spill past her lashes. They skidded down her cheeks. So much for her newly applied layer of makeup!

She watched as he awkwardly turned away and slowly shuffled from the room. Then she whirled around to confront Titus. "How soon can you set up an appointment with that sketch artist Rhys was talking about?" Her heart was pounding so badly that she feared it might explode.

Titus took one look at her face and hurried to the credenza on the side of the room to pour her a cup of coffee. "Possibly as soon as tomorrow morning. I'll make some calls right away."

She dove for her purse to hunt for a tissue. "We need to find the truck that hit me. Now!" She snapped her fingers. "Yesterday!"

"That's the plan." Titus regarded her in concern.

"I'm going to make him pay," she cried in a low voice, dabbing at her eyes with her tissue, then blowing her nose. "He's going to answer for all the wrongs he's done my family."

"Understood." He crouched down beside her chair. "Can I get you anything else?"

"Justice," she snapped. "I want justice!"

CHAPTER 8: NO TIME FOR ROMANCE

ALORA

The rest of Alora's work day passed in a blur. She kept her appointment for an online conference call with Pierre Landstrom, the acquisitions manager of Pezel, LLC. It felt as if her lips were moving mechanically as she patiently answered his questions about how her company could take his company to the next level in terms of productivity profitability. She'd never before found it so difficult to concentrate on work. Throughout their entire conversation, anxiety burned in her to return to the hospital to meet with her siblings.

She also couldn't wait to see Rhys again. Every time she closed her eyes, she could still feel the imprint of his kisses on her lips. *We're dating.* She was still absorbing that astonishing fact. *I'm actually dating Rhys Calcagni!*

Titus worked right outside her office door all

afternoon, making the calls he'd promised and doing heaven-only-knew what other business on behalf of Rhys and Genesis & Sons in her waiting area. It was still hard to believe that an employee from her biggest rival firm was the one working so hard to ensure her safety. It should have been a DRAW employee. Unfortunately, she no longer knew where the loyalties of their own security team lay, since the dangers swirling ever nearer seemed to be coming from inside their own ranks.

Her new executive assistant, Shep Peterson, an aspiring account representative who was studying for his M.B.A., fielded her ever-ringing phone line. He also handled her wildly active email inbox and social media accounts. He'd proven himself proficient in weeding out the non-essential correspondence, redirecting requests and complaints to the appropriate departments and only bringing her the items that truly needed her attention.

Major stealthily patrolled in and out of her office and waiting area via a side door, though she noted he was careful to stay out of the zones covered by her security camera. Thus, Mr. Landstrom of Pezel, LLC had no way of knowing how well guarded she was while they conversed.

Even on conference calls like this, she preferred to work standing up. She slowly paced in front of the floor-to-ceiling window on the west wall that overlooked the Cook Inlet. Mr. Landstrom's face was displayed on the large screen to her left, and the bluetooth microphone secured to her ear made it possible to speak with him as clearly as if he was in the room.

Which didn't prevent her mind from wandering as he rambled on and on about his vision for his company's dog sleds. His animation grew as he explained how the newly engineered runners and stanchions would be lighter weight and more durable, allowing the sleds to bear a much larger weight capacity. Even though Alora was only half listening, her ears red-flagged his comments about weight loads.

The moment he took a breath, she jumped in. "Since your biggest sales potential is in recreational sports, I don't recommend throwing too many research and development dollars into weight capacity. We should focus on speed and durability, Mr. Landstrom." Mainly speed. That was what mattered most in a race, which would entail keeping the materials as light-weight as possible. In her experience, that would force a compromise on durability.

"What if we can have both?" the manager countered in a falsely bright voice. "Then our sleds would stand the chance of capturing more of the market share in Yukon, Nunavut, and the Northwest Territories."

She wrinkled her nose, considering how little market share there was to be had these days in the way of mail deliveries and such that far north. Snow-mobiles and airplanes were making sleds all but obsolete in the cargo-carrying segment of the industry. "We could run the numbers on the viability of producing two separate models," she mused. "One focused on recreational sports and the other on the transport of cargo." She could see neither the practicality nor the profitability in such a move, but it sounded like Mr. Landstrom was going to need hard data to disenamor him of the idea.

"And double our production costs? No thank you," he fumed. "If you'll just take a look at the prototype drawings I've sent to you, I think you'll see—"

"I have," she assured smoothly. So the man *was* aware he was asking for something extraordinary. Well, if it could be done, her oldest brother would figure it out. "I went ahead and turned them over to our company's techno-genius a few days ago. Let me tell you, Greyson Maddox is our secret sauce," she bragged. "I can't wait to introduce the two of you." She pulled up both their electronic calendars on her laptop and swiftly compared their availability. "I could set up our next conference for Friday afternoon, if you'd like. How does three o'clock sound?"

"I was told *you* were the secret sauce there." Mr. Landstrom's voice was sly. "Are you telling me DRAW Corporation has not one, but two, secret sauces?"

"Just one." She smiled. "He's the heart and soul of what we do here. Mark my words, you're going to be impressed when you hear his assessment of your prototypes." He would have them redesigned with every flaw worked out and every imaginable alteration dissected via charts and graphs.

On a sudden burst of inspiration, Alora offered, "If you prefer, I can fly you in to meet with us in person." DRAW desperately needed this contract to bolster their stagnating profit margin. She needed it, as well, to prove to her family they'd made the right choice installing her in her new position.

He paused a moment before his appreciative smile flashed across the large screen. "That would be fantastic, actually."

"Great! I'll have my assistant get in touch with yours to make the arrangements."

A movement in the doorway of Alora's office caught her attention. Titus was standing there. Just like Major had done all afternoon, he was standing just outside the reach of her video camera. He studied Pierre Landstrom's image with an arrested expression on his face. After a moment, Titus pulled out his phone and took a snapshot of the man.

Thoroughly mystified by his actions, Alora said a few more gracious niceties and ended the call. "I know Pierre Landstrom is an interesting character," she chuckled, "but really, Titus? You need a souvenir photo?"

For an answer, he placed a finger over his lips. She watched as he feverishly began to examine her office, pulling books off shelves and shaking small vases. He even climbed on a chair to examine her air duct vent on the wall. She'd watched enough movies to know he was checking for hidden cameras.

"Hey, I appreciate your dedication to your job," she teased, "but isn't that a little much?"

"Turn on some music. I work better that way," he said tersely.

Why certainly, your highness. Let me get right on that. Shaking her head at him, Alora moved to her chrome desk in the center of the room and flipped on her desktop computer. Pulling up a live stream site on the Internet, she inquired in a mocking tone. "Let me guess, you're a hard rock kinda guy?"

"That'll do." He didn't look up.

She turned up the volume and let the sounds of an 80s band fill her office. Any second now, Titus was going to turn around and tell her what was really going on. She tapped the toe of her stiletto impatiently as he pulled a device out of his pocket that resembled a walkie talkie. He extended its antenna and circled the room. Twice. Then he turned off the device, pocketed it, and moved to stand beside her.

He bent his head to speak directly in her ear. "Your friendly Mr. Landstrom is at the Anchorage Airport. Why did you offer to fly him into town?"

"What do you mean?" She frowned at him. "His

company is based in British Columbia." She had to raise her voice to be heard above the music.

"You can turn the music down now."

She complied and described the whereabouts of the company Mr. Landstrom worked for.

"That may be the case, princess, but I'm telling you, those were the Chugach peaks outside the window behind his head."

Her chest felt suddenly cold. "Show me." She'd been working this account since before her car accident. It was a miracle their negotiations had survived her lengthy absence from the office. Landing a contract with Pezel, LLC would be her biggest accomplishment to date as a newly minted CEO.

Titus held out his phone to her. He had the screen zoomed in on Mr. Landstrom's snapshot.

She tapped on the screen and zoomed in further on the mountain range in the background. Her stomach tightened with dread. Titus was correct. It was the Chugach Mountain Range. "I don't understand," she said in a low voice. "I met Mr. Charles Pezel in person at a conference in New York City last fall. It was a solid lead."

"When did you start working with this Mr. Landstrom?" Titus pressed.

She raised and lowered her shoulders, feeling the ache return to her neck from earlier. "Two weeks before my accident, give or take a few days." She squeezed her eyes closed and reopened them as the possibility of a new enemy flitted across her mind, one she hadn't considered before now. She and her siblings had been so focused on Kellan's twin and his shenanigans that they hadn't looked much farther for signs of treachery.

"Titus!" she gasped. "Do you really think—?"

"I don't know," he returned sharply. "May I borrow your computer?" He leaned in, as if preparing to rest his hands on her keyboard, then stopped and pulled back. "Never mind! I need a connection I know is secure. If your systems here at DRAW have been compromised..." He let his words dwindle.

"Compromised?" Alora pressed a hand to her chest, feeling like her world was imploding all over again.

"That's what I'm being paid the big bucks to figure out." He glanced at his watch. "How soon can you be ready to leave?"

"Now." Feeling sick to her stomach, she booted down her computer, stuffed the Pezel file back in her briefcase, and glided toward the door. "I just need to debrief Shep for the day. It won't take long."

"Don't tell him where you're going," Titus advised sharply. "Just say something vague, like..." He waved a hand. "You have something you need to take care of, and you'll see him in the morning."

She shot him an agonized look. "Do you have any

reason to think Shep is mixed up in whatever this is?"

"No, but you can't be too careful."

"Okay." She paused at the door and drew a deep breath. "Okay. More lies forthcoming. I feel like I'm about to throw up." Instead, she was going to have to pretend that everything was normal.

"No time for that." Titus reached around her for the door handle. "Big smile, Miss Maddox. Put on your CEO I-own-the-world strut."

"I do not strut." She gave him a withering look.

"You know what I mean." He smirked as he opened the door for her.

Shep didn't look surprised at Alora's announcement that she was leaving. He eyed Titus with interest and no small amount of admiration as he shuffled a few folders around on his desk. "Your latest messages, Miss Maddox." He handed her the first folder. "In this next folder is a lead on something a little over-the-top that might amount to nothing, but I think it should be your call, considering who it is." He waved the second folder at her.

"Tell me," she urged, "the shortest version possible." If her work with the Pezel account dwindled to nothing, she was going to have to replace it with another viable lead and fast.

"An eccentric scientist named Amancio Belmonte wants to build some exclusively solar, wind, and water powered self-sustaining facility as his final hurrah before retiring. Swears it's the culmination of all his life work." He handed her the second folder. "I'm going to warn you right up front, though." He shook his head. "What the guy has in mind sounds more like a bunker, and his notes read a little too much like the script of *Blast From the Past*, so brace yourself."

"Amancio Belmonte?" A short, incredulous laugh escaped her. "You aren't, by any chance, referring to the gazillionaire extraordinaire oil tycoon Mr. Belmonte from Texas?"

"The one and only." Shep affirmed with a wide grin. "See? Told you it might be worth looking into, even if it's only for entertainment."

"Thanks, Shep. I'll take a look at his notes." They actually sounded pretty fascinating to her, though she wasn't sure she could spare them more than a quick glance this evening. She added the two folders to her already full briefcase. "You have my personal number if anything urgent arises."

"Yes, ma'am, I do." The phone rang. He waved at her and took the call.

It seemed to her that Titus and Major seemed to be hovering a little closer than usual on their short walk to the parking garage.

"Check the undercarriage," Titus snapped.

"I intend to. Wait here," Major ordered at the door. "I'll pull up to the curb." Without waiting for a response, he pushed open the glass door and strode into the parking garage.

In less than a minute, he was nosing her SUV to the curb. The three of them were soon cruising toward the Gjoa Haven Medical Center.

"Please assure me you weren't looking for a car bomb," Alora pleaded faintly.

"No can do, princess." Titus was seated beside her in the backseat, with his hand resting on the holster beneath his blazer. His expression was grim and watchful.

She'd never seen her security team on such full alert. "What can you tell me about what's going on?" She'd come to accept the fact that Titus had secrets. However, she'd also come to trust him.

"You need to warn Greyson. He might be the next target."

A tremulous squeak escaped Alora as she fished in her purse for her cell phone. "What should I tell him?"

"Do you know where he's at right now?"

"Most likely in the lower level labs, but I'll find out."

Titus leaned closer to the door, scanning the streets beyond the window. "Tell him to take a cab straight to the hospital. No using any privately owned vehicles and no detours home."

"We could offer to drive him," she suggested,

trying to tamp down on the alarm snaking its way through her insides.

"We could, but I'd like to live to see another day, and Rhys's orders are for me to keep you alive. That means no getting too cozy with anyone who might be wearing a set of crosshairs on their forehead."

Alora hastily dialed her oldest brother with shaking hands. He picked up right away. "Greyson? Where are you?"

"Work," he supplied in a clipped tone.

"Oh, thank goodness!" she muttered. "Listen, I need you to keep acting like everything is normal, but get to the hospital as fast as you can. Take a cab, please. Don't drive your own car, don't tell anyone where you're going, and no detours. You got it?"

There was a stark silence on the other end of the line. "Is this a joke?" Greyson sounded irritated.

"I wish it was." She pressed two fingers to her throbbing temple. "Greyson, please. I'm begging you." She couldn't bear the thought of anything bad happening to him.

"Okay, fine," he growled. "I'm calling a cab." He disconnected the line.

Titus was already on another call. "Landstrom," he was saying. "I just forwarded you his snapshot." He waved at Alora. "How do you spell the company's name?"

"P-E-Z-E-L."

He repeated the spelling to whoever he was

speaking to. "Yes, based out of British Columbia." He covered his mouthpiece. "What's the nature of the project you were working on for Pezel?"

"Dog sleds," she supplied flatly.

He uncovered his mouthpiece. "Dog sleds, boss. Yep. I'll tell her." He ended the call. "Your boyfriend is asking you not to return home this evening. He's recommending that you stay with Jacey for a few nights."

That shouldn't be a problem. Jacey and Luca had plenty of extra space in which to house a guest. "Slumber party!" Alora shook her arms in the air in a fake hurrah.

Titus looked faintly amused. He directed Major to drop them off at a rear entrance of the hospital, where a man in a security outfit let them in. Titus quickly hustled her up the elevators to the floor where Kellan was being treated. Two bodyguards were posted outside his door.

Rhys was pacing the hall beyond them. At the sight of Alora, he strode in her direction and bent his head to peer in her face. "Thank God you're safe," he muttered.

His dark, wavy hair was tousled as if he'd run his hands through it. Plus, his blazer was missing, and his white shirt sleeves were rolled. She'd never seen this side of him before. He was all-business as he gave orders to his security team and ushered her ahead of him into Kellan's room.

Kellan was lounging in bed, looking a few shades healthier than earlier in the day. His hospital gown had been replaced with a sporty red t-shirt and a pair of board shorts. He looked ready to step onto the beach and hit the waves.

Alora smiled to realize that Kellan was back — truly back. But before she could say anything to him, Rhys held up a hand and barked to her brother, "Look somewhere else!"

"No problem, bro!" With a grin, Kellan picked up a pillow and held it between them, blocking their view of his face. He also turned up the volume on the television. The evening news blared across the room.

With that, Rhys pulled Alora into his arms and sealed his mouth over hers. "I was close to having a stroke while waiting for you to arrive," he muttered between kisses.

She blushed at the knowledge that Rhys was kissing her like he no longer cared who found out he had feelings for her.

"I'm safe." She wrapped her arms around his neck. "Thanks to you."

He pressed his face to her neck and breathed deeply. "I couldn't breathe normally until Titus texted me that you were back in the building." His rich baritone sounded muffled. "It's because I'm so in love with you, Alora."

"You love me?" she whispered, awed.

"I have fallen about as far as a man can fall," he

confessed huskily. "I hope I'm not scaring you by telling you this." He raised his head to gaze anxiously down at her.

"I don't scare easily," she held his gaze steadily. "I care for you, too, Rhys. I'll admit my feelings are new and unexpected. I'm still absorbing everything that's happened between us and around us, so if you can be patient with me—"

"I don't need an answer right now," he assured. "I just need you, more than anything, to stay safe."

"I will. I'll stay with Jacey for a few days, like you asked, until we can figure things out."

"Thank you." He kissed her again.

A double tap sounded on the door.

"That's Titus." He dropped his arms.

"Hold on," she hissed, laying a hand on one arm to detain him. She dug in her purse. She came up with a tissue. "It's for the lipstick." She waved it at him.

He accepted it with a twinkle in his bourbon eyes. "Thanks, love."

She smiled at him. "Gotta take care of my guy."

He pressed a hand to his heart and kissed her with his eyes. Then he moved across the room to open the door, rubbing her lipstick from his mouth as he walked.

Alora was surprised when the volume of the television escalated instead of decreased.

Titus was on the other side of the door; so was

Greyson. He stomped into the room, his bowtie and natty suit more askew than usual. "Would anyone care to tell me what's going on?" He shot an irritated look at Kellan. "Do you mind? I can't hear myself think!"

For an answer, Kellan bumped up the volume a few more ticks.

The sound of an explosion filled the hospital room. Alora and Greyson whirled to stare at the screen, stunned, as the station replayed the video footage a few more times. The news anchor's voice narrated what was happening. "A startling explosion rocked the usually peaceful Coastal Trail side of town, destroying a historic mansion. Authorities on the scene are still trying to determine the cause of the explosion. As the investigation unfolds..."

Kellan finally turned down the television. His face was white as he faced his siblings. "That was your home, Grey."

"That's insane!" Greyson rasped. "This has to be some sort of mad joke."

"I can play it again, if you'd like."

Alora pressed a hand to her chest. "It was your home, Greyson. I'm so sorry."

His shoulders slumped. "I was about to head home early when you called, Alora. My security app had just sent me a notice that one of the cams had detected movement inside the house. Figured it was probably nothing, but..."

She threw her arms around him. It had been something, alright, meaning whatever had motivated Titus to have her call Greyson had likely saved his life.

He hugged her tightly. "It's like someone is trying to wipe every Maddox off the face of the earth."

But why? The dangers closing in on them were much bigger and darker than she'd ever imagined.

CHAPTER 9: GOSSIP GIRLS

ALORA

For the next few days, Alora worked from one of Jacey and Luca's spare bedrooms. Though she missed her office, it was far from a hardship, considering that her youngest sister and her husband lived in a 17,000 square foot Mediterranean-style paradise. It boasted a theater, both indoor and outdoor pools, a bowling alley, a music recording studio, a gym, and a two-story library among other luxurious features. Alora's Tudor-style mansion in the hills was much smaller — not that her impromptu vacation in their home was about comparing her life to theirs. For the thousandth time in the last year and a half, she was just grateful that her wayward youngest sibling had finally found her path.

"Kinda feels like a bit of a role reversal, doesn't it?" Jacey's voice wafted to her from the open bedroom door, which Alora had left ajar for no particular reason.

Alora glanced up from her laptop and smiled. She was perched in the middle of a king-sized guest bed in borrowed gray yoga pants and a black top with spaghetti straps. Her hair was piled in a loose knot atop her head. It was Friday afternoon. Her penciled-in appointment with Pierre Landstrom had come and gone without so much as a phone call from him. In fact, she'd been unable to reach him since the explosion at Greyson's home.

"You were forever bailing me out in my teen years." Jacey stepped farther into the room, blue eyes twinkling with mischief. She was wearing a swanky, floor-length sheath, navy with the outline of a few enormous white diamonds streaking their way across her hip-hugging skirt. When she glided to the window to look out over the gated grounds below, a large, V-shaped cut-out bared her creamy golden shoulders. "And now I finally get to repay you by bailing you out for once."

"I appreciate it." Alora's grin widened. "You look amazing, by the way. Have you come to make me change out of these super comfortable yoga pants for dinner? Because I will, if you insist, although it might be accompanied by a little kicking and screaming."

"It's your choice." Her sister tucked a strand of her long blonde hair behind one ear. "I mean, if you wish to remain looking like a hobo when Rhys joins us for dinner, be my guest, but—"

Alora gave a small shriek of alarm and shot out of bed so quickly that she snagged her foot on the duvet and dragged it with her to the floor.

Jacey burst into laughter. "Well, I was trying to decide how much I was going to pry for an update on where things stand between the two of you, but now I don't need to." She moved across the room to swing open the door to the walk-in closet Alora hadn't spent much time browsing through. "I have a little black dress that looks yummy and a teal-colored cocktail dress, if you prefer some color."

Alora felt a tad dizzy at the thought of seeing Rhys again. "Both sound fantastic. Maybe I should try them on before making a decision." She padded bare foot across the hardwood floor to the coffee station at the wet bar. She poured herself a cup and made no attempt to dilute its potency with cream or sugar. It was one of those take-it-straight kind of days, especially since she sensed a sisterly interrogation was forthcoming.

Jacey emerged from the closet with a dress hanger swinging from each hand. "Here you go, darling." She hung the two dresses from hooks on the wall just outside the closet. A tall, oval antique dressing mirror rested there. "So are you going to make me fish for details or what?"

"About?" Alora teased, knowing full well her

youngest sister was angling for information about her relationship with Rhys.

"Begging it is." Jacey whirled in her direction, her hands clasped beseechingly in front of her. Her wedding diamond flashed like fire in the rosy light pouring through the picture window from the setting sun. "Oh, please, please, please tell me how the mightiest-of-all-mighty Maddox sisters fell off her ivory pedestal and landed beneath the devastating charm of yet another Calcagni man. I really want to know," she finished with a breathless giggle. "Oh, come on!" she exploded when Alora didn't start talking right away. "Rhys Calcagni, of all people? When did this happen, and why have you been holding out on me?"

Alora bit her lower lip. "I really don't know," she confessed. "How did you find out, by the way?"

"Oh, I don't know." Jacey rolled her eyes. "He only stops by the house to check on you fifty million times per day. Not to check on Greyson, who is also staying with us. Just you." Her blue eyes glinted with keen interest. "Then there's the way his expression goes all puppy dog soft every time he hears your name. Seriously, Alora! What spell did you cast on the guy? A few weeks ago, he was my serious-as-death-and-taxes, number-crunching COO of a brother-in-law, and now he's..."

"He's what?" Alora asked quickly.

"In love," Jacey retorted, "with you. I ask again. When did this happen?"

Alora wrapped her arms around her middle as she surveyed the two lovely dresses hanging on the wall. "Over a few insults we traded back in high school, apparently, or so he says." She still couldn't believe Rhys had been crushing on her for that long.

"Omigosh! Tell me everything!" Jacey flounced down on the loveseat in the bay window that served as a lounge.

So Alora did — right down to how the man holding her hand in the hospital had likely pulled her back from death, itself. She downed her entire cup of coffee while doing so and returned the empty cup to the bar.

"That is the most romantic thing I've ever heard." Jacey's eyes were misty and her hands crossed on her chest by the time Alora finished her story.

"Right. Says the woman who's married to Luca Calcagni," Alora chuckled. Even after marrying her sister, the man had scored a few centerfold features in the tabloids, touted as one of the swooniest men alive.

"Fine. Correction. Your love story is the most romantic thing in the world, second only to Luca Calcagni."

They both laughed.

When Jacey spoke again, her voice was hushed.

"Seriously, though, are you ready for this, Alora?" She shook her head. "Having a Calcagni man in your life isn't the same as having a regular guy. They're intense and possessive and..." She waved her hands at flaming cheeks. "I guess I'm trying to say that they're all-in when it comes to the women they love."

Don't I know! Alora made a faint moaning sound, trying to figure out how to put her feelings into words. "There's no going back for me, Jace. What's happening between him and me is really happening."

"Then I'm a thousand shades happy for you. I really am." Jacey blinked rapidly, dabbing at the corners of her eyes. "You happen to be two of the most wonderful people in the universe. If anyone I know has ever deserved to be happy, it's you." She gave a small bounce of excitement on the love seat. "So when are you going to tell the world and set a date to tie the knot? All that jazz..."

"I don't know," Alora answered more sharply than she intended. "Not yet — that I can tell you."

"Oh, Alora!" Jacey sighed, leaning forward so that her elbows rested on her knees. She cupped her face in her hands and stared beseechingly across the room at her oldest sister. "Please tell me you're not going to let that age-old family feud garbage stand in the way of your happiness. You're better than that."

Alora slapped her hands on her hips. "I'm the CEO of their biggest rival firm. Criticize me all you wish, but this isn't a simple matter, Jace. Besides, my relationship with Rhys is new. We need time to date and gel and move forward as a couple — a luxury we may not get any time soon with all the danger and intrigue spinning around our heads."

Jacey's mouth formed an O of shock. "So you're going to risk losing him, just because things are a little tough right now?"

"No, sweetie, I'm not." Alora's chest felt cold at the mere thought. "You asked me why I've been holding out on you. Well, this is why. Because I knew I wouldn't have the answers you wanted, and I wasn't head-over-heels in love with the idea of you thinking less of me for it." She sighed. "Sometimes older sisters like to keep one hip firmly planted on the ivory pedestal, alright?"

"Fair enough, but where does this leave you and Rhys?" Jacey moaned, clasping her hands to her cheeks.

"I don't know, Jace. I truly don't know." Alora would give anything right now to have an answer to that question. It had been burning a hole through her heart for days. "All I can tell you is I'm the CEO of a firm under attack from a silent enemy, who may or may not be gunning for every member of my family," she drew a deep breath before adding, "for reasons I do not yet understand." She shook her head. "It means I'm not in the position to simply do things that make me happy. I have the wellbeing of too many others to consider, too many people depending on me for their jobs, paychecks, and other benefits — none of which is going to be easy to provide if our stock price continues to tank."

The price of DRAW Corporation shares had hit a ten-year low at the close of market the day after the explosion that had leveled Greyson's home. Dozens of articles had been written and published since then by investment analysts about the instability of senior leadership at DRAW. They'd even managed to get their hands on Kellan's lesser known story about his boating accident. Calling it a run of bad luck, the analysts had subsequently lowered their ratings on the firm from the solid A it had always held to a B+. Not only was it at an all-time low in the history of DRAW Corporation, it had happened under her watch.

Silence settled between them, during which Alora decided she would be wearing the teal halter dress to dinner. It had full, swirly skirts that would land just above her knees, and it would be different from all the somber dark and neutral colors she tended to wear to work.

"Just promise me one thing." Jacey stood with a sigh.

"What's that?" Alora reached for the teal dress and withdrew it from the hook to lay it across the guest bed.

"Save a little room for happiness somewhere in that crazy busy CEO schedule of yours, okay?"

"I'm trying, Jace."

"Nice girls don't always have to finish last."

"You think I'm nice?" Alora chuckled as she gathered up her toiletries for a quick shower. "Boy, do I have you fooled!"

"It's just that you've always taken care of everybody else." Jacey's tone was wistful. "Maybe it's time you let someone else take care of you."

Alora shot a grin over her shoulder as she headed for the bathroom. "I don't think you need to worry about that. Like Luca, family means everything to Rhys. I'm super lucky that all the deep-seated loyalty and honor the Calcagni men possess seems to extend to their girlfriends."

"Oo, now *you're* fishing for information," Jacey called gayly after her.

"Shamelessly." Alora closed the bathroom door but finished their gossip fest from the other side of the wooden panels as she peeled out of her clothing. "Rumor has it that Knox Calcagni has been spending a lot of time with Priss." Priscilla Cardale was Bailey's office manager.

"Bah!" Jacey scoffed. "You might not want to get your hopes up too high on their behalf. Knox is a bit of a player. He's got a mean streak, too — nearly scalded my knee off with his coffee when I first returned to town." She'd come home a widow when

Easton, the Calcagni's youngest brother, suffered a fatal crash during a NASCAR race. She'd also come home pregnant with Easton's son, though she hadn't realized that fact until weeks later. Alora had always suspected it was the biggest reason Luca had whee-dled Jacey into a marriage of convenience, which had very quickly turned into one of passionate love. Luca was utterly enchanted with his bride, and Jacey worshipped the ground he walked on.

Alora smiled at Jacey's description of Knox's mean streak, wondering if there was any truth to it. She knew her younger sister hadn't been quickly or easily accepted by the Calcagnis upon her return to Alaska. Over time, they'd grown to accept her, though, and eventually to adore her. No doubt their acceptance of Jacey would make Alora's path into their lives smoother when the time came to go public with her and Rhys's relationship.

She turned the shower on full blast and gloried in the blast of water that cascaded over her. Despite the sizzling temperature of the water, she shivered at the thought of seeing Rhys again. She hadn't yet told him she loved him. She was still trying to sort through her feelings for him. They were unexpected and confusing. He was such a complex creature — brilliant and powerful, possessive and adoring. He was a man capable of keeping her safe, melting her insides with his kisses, and keeping her emotions in one big, chaotic tangle.

It wasn't something she felt she could ever fully explain to Jacey, but her relationship with Rhys wasn't really a matter of whether or not she had feelings for the man. She did. It was more a matter of having so many feelings for him that she was at risk of losing herself in them. She might not have much experience with the emotion called love, but she'd watched way too many others mishandle it and let it destroy them, particularly her professional friends. Too many women made too many sacrifices for love; and, when the honeymoon was over, they found themselves walking in their husbands' shadows — a bundle of bitterness and malcontent.

Alora had no interest in folding her ambitions beneath those of any man, no matter how wonderful he was. She didn't ever want to experience the resentment or hatred that would follow such a mistake. If there was ever going to be a place in her life for love, it needed to be the love of a man who could accept all of her. The woman *and* the CEO. And if she couldn't find such a man, logic told her she was better off alone. She'd grown accustomed to the loneliness at the top. It was nothing new to her.

The teal dress waiting for her on the guest bed, however, did represent something new. Alora tugged the ends of her bath towel more firmly around her as she surveyed it. It was far more fun and frivolous than the outfits she normally wore to social gatherings. If she wore it downstairs to the dining room, there was the risk that others, besides Jacey, would suspect something in her love life had changed.

Ultimately, she decided to wear the dress and risk her heart. She couldn't wait to see the expression on Rhys's face when he saw her in it. Her heartbeat raced in anticipation as she dabbed on her makeup and styled her hair.

As it turned out, he didn't wait for her to enter the dining room. He was standing at the bottom of the long, circular stairs when she glided down them.

He was wearing a camel colored suit and a white dress shirt that was unbuttoned at the collar. It might very well be the first time she'd ever seen him without a tie. His jaw was smooth from a recent shave, and his dark, wavy hair was combed back from his forehead. The faint scent of his aftershave wafted over her.

"You are so beautiful." He crooked his arm at her.

She blushed at the uncloaked admiration in his eyes and obligingly laid her arm on his. He tucked it more firmly around his arm and leaned closer. "The dress isn't bad, either, love. Matches your eyes."

"You clean up pretty good, yourself." She tipped her face up to his, and he swooped in for a lingering kiss that stole her breath and made her knees weak.

"Before you fret, there's no one around. I made sure of it," he muttered against her lips.

"In that case," she sighed. She stood on her

tiptoes to wrap her arms around his neck. The stresses of the last few days evaporated beneath the warm pressure of his mouth moving against hers and the cherishing clasp of his hands on her waist. "I've missed you, Rhys."

"I've missed you, too." He deepened his next kiss, pulling her deeper into the enchantment weaving its way around them.

It wasn't that they hadn't seen each other the past few days, but they had not enjoyed a single moment alone until now. Now that Alora was finally back in the circle of his arms, she wanted to stay there...forever.

"Call me cautious," she sighed when he raised his head a fraction, "but I'd rather have at least a tiny scrap of privacy for what I'm about to say next, so please." She tugged on his hands. "Humor me."

She walked backwards with him into the nearest room, which happened to be the library.

He followed, not letting go of her hands or dropping her gaze until they were inside the dimly lit room. He let go of her hand only long enough to shut the door. Then he leaned his shoulders against it and pulled her close again.

"I'm falling for you," she confessed in a tremulous voice, "and it terrifies me."

His bourbon gaze leaped with joy. "I'm here to catch you." He reached up to trail a finger down her cheek. "You know that."

"I just..." She stopped and bit her lip.

"Yes?" A curious smile tugged at the corners of his mouth.

"A conversation with my sister earlier. Jacey knows about us now." She made a wry sound. "She sorta guessed on her own, and I didn't see any point in denying it."

"I like the sound of that." He leaned in to brush his lips against hers once more.

"I think she's afraid I'm going to break your heart."

"Are you?" Though his expression was lazy and indulgent on the surface, she knew it was a loaded question.

"I don't want to hurt you, Rhys — not now or ever!" The very thought filled her with agony.

"Then I don't see the problem."

"I do!" The words tore themselves from her. "Jacey is right. The way things currently stand between us is not the least fair to you."

He looked surprised. "Ah...I'm afraid I'm not following."

She shook her head in frustration. "I'm not blind to the fact that you're doing most of the giving here, and I'm doing most of the receiving."

His mouth quirked. "I don't have any complaints, Alora. I knew what I was getting into when I decided to pursue you."

"I just want you to know that I don't plan to keep you waiting forever."

He nipped at the corner of her mouth. "Just for the record, I don't plan to let you."

Her heart tipped dizzily in her chest. "You are the best thing that's ever happened to me, Rhys."

"Ah, hold that thought." He dug in his pocket for his cell phone and clicked a few buttons. "Mind repeating that so I can record it?"

"Why?" A surprised chuckle escaped her.

"So I can replay it to you after we have our first fight."

"You are despicable!" she hissed, trying not to laugh.

"No, I'm the best. You just said so, yourself."

"I just wish I could tell the rest of the world about you." She searched his face anxiously. "About us."

His tender expression didn't change. "Neither of us expected this to be easy."

"No, it's not." She wound her arms around his neck again. "Kiss me one more time, Rhys, before we have to return to the big, bad, real world."

CHAPTER 10: UNEXPECTED DINNER GUESTS

RHYS

Guilt stabbed Rhys as he claimed Alora's lips. He honestly had no concerns about her breaking his heart. Quite the opposite. It was more likely he was going to end up breaking hers.

A note of desperation crept into his kiss, as his fear of losing her grew. In the coming days, he knew his actions were going to test the delicate bonds of trust he'd so painstakingly worked to build between them.

His conversation with Luca earlier in the day about tender offers, proxy fights, and poison pills was making his chest ache. He didn't like keeping secrets from Alora, but now was not the time to burden her with more than she was already dealing with. She was still recovering from life-threatening injuries. Kellan was still recovering from head trauma. Greyson had just lost his home and nearly all his earthly possessions. Plus, each of the Maddox siblings continued to grapple with how to handle the matter of Kellan's twin.

Unfortunately, the market wasn't showing their company any mercy in the meantime. There were no time-outs in the cut-throat world of business. No pause buttons to hit.

Though a robust and profitable company in the past, DRAW Corporation stock was severely under-valued at the moment, making them ripe for a hostile takeover. He and Luca were watching the market carefully, identifying the hawks that were starting to circle the firm. It was only a matter of time before a group of investors attempted to buy up the common stock and force a change of leadership at the board level.

Luca had finally suggested the most obvious solution a few hours ago — that Genesis & Sons might ought to throw their hat into the ring to engineer the buyout themselves. He claimed it only made sense if Rhys intended to marry Alora, anyway. It certainly made sense on paper. Genesis had the necessary capital, the depth of human resources, and the kind of leadership it would take to pull it off.

As Rhys kissed Alora, he knew his company had the power and capacity to purchase her family's company, whether she approved of his actions or not. That, in fact, such a move on his and Luca's part might be the only way to save her flailing company at this juncture. Depending on how she interpreted his actions, however, it could cost him her trust and affection forever.

He longed, more than anything, for honesty and transparency between them. Those were the only sure things on which to build the kind of relationship he wanted with her — the kind that would last.

In the past few hours, he'd debated every imaginable possibility for how to keep Alora in his life, considering what he and Luca were planning next. He'd drawn up actual charts, calculated probabilities, and made projections. Only one solution stood a chance of weathering the storm that was coming their way.

"Marry me!" The words tore from deep within him. It wasn't the debonair, romantic declaration he would have made, given more time, but they might not have more time. He felt like it was a now-or-never moment.

She drew back in astonishment, gripping his shoulders and looking dazed. "What did you say?"

"I want you to marry me." He pushed away from the door and pivoted with her so he could take a knee in front of her. "To be my wife, my best friend, and the keeper of my secrets for the rest of our lives."

"You do realize we're still not in the position to go public with our relationship," she murmured, still looking dazed.

"Then marry me in secret. Be my wife, Alora. Just be mine."

"I—" she stammered, blushing furiously. "Yes." Her eyelashes fluttered against her cheeks.

He shot to his feet with a joyful cry, lifted her in his arms, and spun her around. His eyes were damp when he set her back on her feet. "Thank you for saying yes." His voice was rough with emotion. "I didn't know it was possible to be this happy."

"Me, neither."

As Rhys leaned in to kiss his new fiancée, somewhere in the back of his mind, he registered the fact that she'd not once told him that she loved him — yet. He could only hope and pray that, in time, she would grow to love him even a fraction of how much he already loved her. Until that time came, his love for her would have to be enough for them both.

"I have a ring I'd like you to have, even if you're not ready to wear it yet," he informed her softly. "It's a family heirloom."

"I can't wait to see it." Her voice held a dreamy quality.

"It's in a gold setting, which some might say is a little dated, so feel free to make any changes you want. Reset it or modernize it. It's entirely up to you."

"I like the color gold." She smoothed a hand over his lapel. "Most of my jewelry is gold."

"So I've noticed."

"And I adore old things," she continued. "So many of them were made better, back in the day. Made to last."

He caught her hand and pressed it against his heart. "I want us to last."

"So do I."

Three simple words, but they gave him hope.

"I'm not ready to join the others for dinner," he confessed, toying with her fingers against his chest. "I want you all to myself for a little longer. Is that selfish?"

She shrugged, her blue-green eyes glowing in the light from the setting sun. "If I agree, does that make me selfish, too?" she teased.

"Maybe it's not such a cardinal sin if we're selfish together." He reached up to cup her face and slowly lowered his head to hers once more. Nipping little kisses from her earlobe to her chin, he finally sealed his mouth over hers. It was a long time before he raised his head again. By then, the sun was nearly finished setting.

He gazed past her at the room that was fast settling into shadows and experienced more contentment than he'd felt in a long time. It was a gorgeous library with dark wood paneling and ornate trim. Rhys had been inside it many times, but it had never seemed more gorgeous than this evening. Having Alora in his arms in her flirty teal dress turned the room to sheer magic.

"How soon will you marry me?" he asked, lifting a fiery lock of hair from her shoulder. It was as supple and silky as it looked.

"How soon can you secure a license?" she countered, making his heart pound in anticipation.

"We can apply tomorrow. Then there's a three-day waiting period, so you could become Mrs. Rhys Calcagni as soon as mid-week next week."

"I'd like to keep Maddox as my middle name like Bailey did." It wasn't a question.

"Works for me." He wound the red-gold strand of hair around his finger and gave it a gentle tug. "That should give you time to draw up any additional agreements you wish for me to sign."

"A prenuptial, huh?" she mused in an odd voice.

"I'll sign one if you want me to." He had no intention of asking her to do the same.

"Another Maddox and Calcagni merger." She gave a soft laugh, giving him no indication about her opinion on the topic of prenuptial agreements. "Do you think the world is ready for this?"

"There's only one way to find out." At the term *merger*, his chest tightened. It was a reminder that he was about to do something she might consider an unforgivable betrayal. He could only hope that promising her his heart, name, and wealth in advance would be enough to sway her loyalty back in his direction when the time came.

A commotion in the hallway outside the library bought their silence. Rhys heard Jacey's voice.

"She's not in her room. I checked."

"She didn't mention a last-minute meeting." Greyson sounded worried. "Let me try calling her again."

"Well, wherever she is, she's wearing a teal party dress," Jacey announced emphatically. "That I can tell you."

Alora's phone buzzed inside the purse she had strapped over her shoulder.

Rhys chuckled silently. "What do you want to do?" he whispered.

She rolled her eyes and retrieved her phone.

Too bad! Grinning, he reached out to turn on the main light switch to the room. Warm light flooded the library from a series of stained glass wall sconces.

Alora punched a button on the face of her phone to accept the call. "Hello. Alora Maddox speaking."

"Where are you?" her oldest brother exploded.

"In the library," she returned calmly. "Rhys and I had some business to discuss."

"That's funny," he muttered.

"You don't sound like you're laughing," she teased.

"It's just that I'm standing right outside the library, and I could've sworn there was no light on in there a minute ago."

Rhys swiftly moved across the room to drape his forearm against the fireplace mantle.

The door to the library burst open so suddenly that it made Alora jolt.

Greyson's gaze swept between the two of them and grew suspicious. Shaking his head, he raised his voice and tossed over his shoulder, "Found them!"

Jacey skidded into the room seconds later with her infant son, Race, cuddled against her shoulder. "We've been looking all over for you!" she chided. Her eyes twinkled knowingly, first at Rhys, then at her sister. "You don't write. You don't call."

Greyson snorted. "She said they had business to discuss."

"Ah. Business." When Alora's arms stretched out, Jacey promptly handed over the baby. She'd named him Easton after her first Calcagni husband — may he rest in peace — but she called him by his middle name, Race.

Rhys had always liked the name. It felt like a fitting tribute to the brother they'd loved so dearly and lost too soon. He watched indulgently as the two women cooed over and played with Race until the babe smiled and batted the air with his fists.

"He's so precious!" Alora smoothed a hand over the babe's silky head, making Rhys's heart twist with longing. Someday, he wanted a family of his own... with her. It's not something they'd had the opportunity to discuss yet, but a man could dream.

He strode across the room to join the happy huddle. "How's my nephew doing?"

"He's spoiled like you wouldn't believe." Jacey tickled Race's belly, making him laugh. It was one of the most beautiful sounds Rhys had ever heard, second only to the soft little sounds Alora made when he was kissing her. "All he has to do is squeak or point, and Britt jumps to do the little prince's bidding." Britt was the babe's Dutch nanny.

"Oh, boy!" Greyson exclaimed as he scrolled through his text messages.

"That sounds ominous." Alora shot a laughing glance at him over the baby's head.

"Maybe. Maybe not." He ran a hand through his red hair, standing it on end. "According to Bailey, who stopped by the hospital for a visit on her way here, Kellan has decided to check himself out against doctor's orders."

"Why? Is everything okay?" Rhys asked quickly.

"Probably." Greyson made a sound of irritation. "It's Kellan we're talking about here. He's been going stir-crazy stuck in that room for so long." He huffed out a breath. "I should have seen this coming. We all should have."

"Well, he can stay here as long as he likes," Jacey assured. "We have plenty of room. The more, the merrier." She looked genuinely happy at the prospect.

Rhys knew it was partly because she'd been

estranged from her family for the better part of five years after marrying his youngest brother. She was overjoyed at having them back. Well, some of them, anyway. To the best of his understanding, her parents and grandparents still weren't speaking to her. They'd not yet forgiven her for the sin of marrying not one, but two, Calcagni men. Then Jacey's next older sister had gone and married Luca's best friend, Don Kappelman, only a slightly lesser sin in their eyes.

It was going to kill them when they found out their oldest daughter — their CEO, no less — had also fallen prey to the charms of a Calcagni man. It was going to be a fallout of nuclear proportions.

The doorbell rang.

"It's Kellan and his entourage." Luca appeared outside the library and strode past the entrance toward the front door.

"Keep Race entertained a sec, please!" Jacey hurried to join her husband at the door.

Before opening it, he leaned down and gave her a very thorough kiss.

Over the past several months, Rhys had been eaten alive with envy over what his oldest brother had with his wife. Tonight was the first time he could remember not feeling anything but happiness for them.

"I love you," Jacey said softly, touching his cheek when he lifted his head to gaze deeply into her eyes.

"Don't ever stop, *cara*."

Rhys waited a beat before joining them in the entry foyer, so as not to intrude on their tender moment.

Luca opened the door.

Bailey reached out to hug Luca the moment she stepped inside the entry foyer. Luca and Don slapped each other on their shoulders. Kellan neatly sidestepped the entire group. "I'm kinda new to this Maddox-Calcagni alliance, so I'll be skipping the sloppy kisses, if you don't mind."

"Not even for me?" Rhys threw out his hands in mock outrage. "Your trusted pilot?"

His words were met with chuckles from most of those gathered and a smirk from Kellan.

"How about a fist bump, instead, bro?" Kellan swung his fist in an arc.

Rhys popped his knuckles lightly against his future brother-in-law's. "How's the melon holding up?"

Kellan shrugged as if it didn't matter. "Eh...if you don't count the headaches, dizziness, nausea, unexplained bouts of sleepiness, and an occasional blank spot in my memory where I find myself standing in the middle of the room in my boxers with no memory of how I got there, I feel tremendous." He gave them a collective air high-five. "At the top of my game, in fact. Someone, toss me a basketball."

He looked healthy and relaxed in tan trousers

and a navy sports jacket. No tie. Like a guy ready to swing by the country club for a beverage after work.

"Oh, grow up already," Alora teased, stepping into the foyer. She was still cuddling Race. "You know the rule. No throwing balls in the house."

"My Grecian vase appreciates that," Luca noted dryly. His arm was loosely slung around Jacey.

She tipped her head against his shoulder to gaze up at him. "Is it really from Greece, darling?"

"No, I lied. It's from K-Mart like everything else we own." He leaned over to kiss her on the mouth.

"Good." She gave an exaggerated sigh. "You do not want to know how many times I've almost knocked it over."

"You're right. I don't." He didn't look overly concerned, though. "Well, now that everyone is here," he cast a sly glance in Rhys's direction, "and all business negotiations concluded for the evening, how about we adjourn to the dining room?"

Rhys hung back so he could enjoy the sight of Alora walking ahead of him. Man, but she looked as much at ease with her young nephew tucked against her shoulder as she did with a briefcase in hand. She was truly an amazingly brilliant, phenomenally talented, multi-faceted woman!

"Don't think for a second I bought that line about discussing business with my sister earlier," Greyson growled at his elbow.

Rhys was so sure he hadn't been standing there a

few seconds ago, that he immediately suspected Greyson had cornered him on purpose. "If you're feeling left out," Rhys teased, "you and I could haggle out something right here and now in the hallway."

"I see the way you look at her," Greyson yanked on his bow tie in irritation, knocking it more askew than usual, "and the way she looks at you." His upper lips curled. "What's with you Calcagni men? You're like a special brand of crack where my sisters are concerned."

Rhys held back a laugh. He'd been accused of worse. "I'm in love with her." Rhys saw no point in being anything less than honorable with his future brother-in-law.

"Yeah?" Greyson's brows rose in a challenge. "Well, that statement, made in the wrong room before the wrong people, could ruin her."

"I'm well aware." It saddened Rhys to realize that the wrong room he was referring to was likely the board room at DRAW Corporation, and the wrong people were his own parents and grandparents. Although Rhys's family was far from perfect, they were much more unified than the Maddoxes.

"Then that's all I have to say on the topic." Greyson's shoulders relaxed. "It's getting harder and harder to hate you, considering everything you've done for my family in recent weeks."

"Glad to hear it." Rhys's heart twisted, knowing

it would get easier to hate him all over again in the coming days. But that was a problem for another day. Since there were so many people in the room who knew about his feelings where Alora was concerned, he saw no reason to torture himself by sitting anywhere else but beside her.

She looked surprised but not disappointed. The moment grace was said and the food was passed, Britt breezed into the room to sweep Race from Alora's arms. She blew the babe a goodbye kiss and proceeded to push her salad around her plate with her fork.

Since he wasn't any more hungry than she was, he reached beneath the table for her hand. Her expression softened, and he knew that she was remembering.

About halfway through the meal, Knox joined them. His gaze passed curiously over those gathered but seemed to linger the longest on Rhys and Alora. Then he took a spare seat at the end of the table and dug into the feast. There were steak medallions drenched in gravy, rotisserie chicken, and roast duck with orange sauce, in addition to an array of salads and sides.

When their group was nearly finished dining, Luca reached for his phone and stared at the screen with an arrested expression. "Looks like we're about to have more company." He handed his phone to Jacey.

"Grandfather!" she exclaimed. "What is he doing here?"

Alora's fingers tightened to a death grip on Rhys's hand under the table.

"I think his reasons for being here," Luca returned slowly, "are secondary to what he will find out if we allow him inside the front door." He glanced around the table, meeting every startled and wary gaze. "However, that doesn't change the fact that he is family and deserves to know what we've chosen to keep from him." His gaze landed on Kellan and remained there. "If you want me to turn Mr. Maddox away, speak up now or forever hold your peace, because I am inclined to open the door to my wife's grandfather."

Jacey's lush mouth was turned down in a grimace. To the best of Rhys's knowledge, Jacey hadn't spoken to her grandfather since the day she'd eloped with his youngest brother, and that was going on seven years ago.

Silence met Luca's statement. "I'll take that as my answer." He held up his phone and spoke into the mouth piece. "Mr. Maddox, this is Luca Calcagni speaking. Welcome to our home. My wife and I will meet you at the front entrance."

Jensen Maddox snarled something unintelligible.

Luca stood and held out his hand to Jacey. "Ready, *bella?*"

Tight-lipped, she rose and placed her hand in

his. "If he rolls up in a tank, I'm going to run and scream like a girl."

"Duly noted." He raised her fingers to his lips and kissed them.

Several tense minutes passed, in which those remaining in the dining room either pretended to eat or gave up, altogether. Only Kellan continued to plow his way with real gusto through his meal.

"What are you all staring at?" He glanced up at one point with his mouth full, chewed, and swallowed. "I'm recovering from hospital food. Don't judge me."

He was tipping up his glass of sparkling berry water when Jensen Maddox stormed into the room. The elder man was a sight to behold in a herringbone suit, a coffee-colored beret, and a quirky orange bowtie. Since Rhys had never suffered through much interaction with the incendiary bedrock of the Maddox clan, he'd never paid too much attention to what the man wore. However, he suddenly understood where Greyson Maddox got his eclectic mix of artistic nerdiness when it came to clothing styles. More notably, the man looked ready to pop one of the bulging veins in his neck.

Rhys braced himself to catch the fellow if and when he imploded.

Jensen Maddox slowly took in the inhabitants around the dining room table, absorbing in slow degrees that the latest generation of Maddoxes and

Calcagnis were not engaged in the same war as the older generations. His face waxed redder and redder as his fury mounted. "What in the blazes is going on here?" His tirade abruptly halted as his gaze landed at last on Kellan. His lined features went chalky with disbelief.

"Kellan?" His voice cracked.

CHAPTER 11: SHOWDOWN

ALORA

A dazed sheen of emotion passed over her grandfather's vision like a cloud, as he swayed in his fancy wingtips.

Horror rose in Alora's throat when she realized he was close to collapsing. She pushed back her chair and shot to her feet, but Rhys was quicker.

He reached the elderly man's side the second he started sagging.

"Here." Kellan, who was sitting the closest, stood and held out the gilded armchair at the foot of the table.

Rhys gently lowered him by his elbows into it. He and Kellan crouched together in front of the older man.

"Get him a drink," Kellan shouted.

Alora moved to stand behind her grandfather.

She reached around the high-back chair to rest her hands on his shoulders.

He reached up to grip one of her hands. "This was the real reason you cried when I told you about Kellan's head injury." His voice was accusing.

"Yes." Her voice was whispery with emotion. She bent to press a kiss to his cheek. "You were entirely correct about the head injury, by the way. Kellan — the real Kellan — was convalescing in the Gjoa Haven Medical Center's rehabilitation wing at the time."

"I see. Or at least I'm trying to." Her grandfather closed his eyes momentarily. When he reopened them, Alora winced at the shame-laced anger she read deep in their depths.

"Who is he?" he demanded. "The other one?"

"Kellan's biological twin, apparently." She moved around the side of the chair to get a better look at her grandfather.

Rhys quickly grabbed a spare chair from the side of the room and pulled it over to her. He angled his head at her, encouraging her to sit.

Her gaze locked on his and held for an extended moment while she settled into the chair, long enough to make her heart beat erratically.

Jensen's eyes traveled between the two of them and hardened. "Apparently, there is much I have missed in recent days." He reached for the glass Jacey handed him and gulped down a few swallows.

"Now!" He sat the glass down on the end of the table with the force of a judge pounding his gavel. "I'd like someone to explain to me why in tarnation that-that..." he pointed a shaking finger in the general direction of DRAW Corporation, "poser is still running free? I want him arrested immediately!"

"Because he's family." Alora touched the top of his hand, but he shook it off.

"He is not!" her grandfather retorted harshly. "He's a criminal who I plan to prosecute to the full extent of the law." He shook his head back and forth like a mangy dog. "My attorneys are going to have a heyday with this one."

Alora continued in a smooth voice, well accustomed to his crotchetiness. "We'd first like to find out his real name, where he's from, and what he wants from us."

"I think that's obvious enough!" her grandfather snarled. "He wants to *be* one of us. He wants to take Kellan's place."

"So it appears. Did you know Kellan had a twin?" she pressed. "Did our parents know?"

"I don't know. Why are you interrogating me, instead of calling the police?" His bushy gray brows drew together in fury. "Seems to me they should be interrogating *him*."

Alora glanced at Rhys, more than ready for him to step in.

"Are you sure?" he mouthed.

She nodded and leaned closer to Jensen Maddox. "Grandfather, this is Rhys Calcagni." She waved in her fiancé's direction. "He's going to explain the details of our current investigation." She hated putting Rhys on the spot, knowing her grandfather wouldn't hesitate to spew his venom on him, but she also knew by now that Rhys possessed broad, emotional shoulders. He could handle it. He would be related to her grandfather, at any rate, when they married. *You don't get to choose your family. Sorry, sweetheart.*

The elder man's upper lip curled in disdain, but he maintained a seething silence as his gaze fell darkly on Rhys.

"My head of security has a contact in the FBI," Rhys notified him in an all-business tone. "They're running the specs of Kellan's twin through some databases. So far, he hasn't popped in any public records, which is highly unusual. Is there any information you can give us to help in the search? The name of the adoption agency you used, for example?"

"Why should I help you?" the older man rasped.

"Because Kellan's twin may have had something to do with my accident," Alora interjected firmly.

"And the explosion that destroyed my home." Greyson had risen at his grandfather's entrance into the dining room, but he remained standing halfway down the dinner table, with his toe of his dress shoe resting on the seat of his chair. His forearms were resting on his knee, his body canted in their direction.

Kellan waved his fork at them. "Well, he certainly had something to do with my current situation."

"Mine, too." Bailey's voice rang in soft, melodic tones across the tense atmosphere of the room. Don's large arm was slung across the back of her chair. He fiddled with a strand of her long, dark hair as she spoke. "I think, in hindsight, most of us would now agree I was all but tossed out of DRAW Corporation on my backside. I'm very fortunate that my husband was able to purchase Titan Industries to safeguard the interests of our family and our company." She leaned in to him, resting a hand on his chest. He dipped his head to brush his lips against her temple.

It was apparent to anyone who was watching them how in love they were. Alora tasted a spurt of envy at the fact that they no longer had to hide their feelings for each other. Like Jacey, Bailey had endured the ostracism of their family when she chose to marry for love. Alora hoped and dreamed that someday she and Rhys would be able to enjoy that same privilege. She didn't know how or when, though. There was no way her parents or grandparents were going to support her upcoming marriage to

Rhys. Not in a million years. It might actually get her voted right out of her position as CEO.

Alora ducked her head to smooth the bouncy folds of skirt that had ridden up her knees a bit. There was going to come a day — she could sense it and was already dreading it — when she would have to make the same decision her sisters had. Because of her family's ruthless ambitions, they would make her choose between them and him. They would never allow her to have both.

She lifted her head to meet Rhys's gaze, knowing what her heart wanted. He gave her a nearly imperceptible nod of reassurance, which made her feel guilty at the knowledge that she still wasn't a hundred percent sure about how to move forward with their relationship. She was agreeing to marry him in secret, with no plan for when she would finally be able to unveil their union to their families or to the public. She was asking him to walk in the shadows with her, indefinitely. He claimed he was willing, but it was something that had the potential to become a real problem for them over time.

Unfortunately, she wasn't in the position to simply choose her personal happiness over everything else. Her decisions — even her personal ones — affected so many others besides herself. At the very least, her decisions affected the lives of Greyson, Bailey, Kellan, and Jacey. Without her at the head of the board table at DRAW, for example, a simple vote could terminate their 10-year marketing contract with Titan Industries. Sure, there would be penalties for DRAW to pay, but both companies would lose revenue in the long run.

Alora breathed in to clear her thoughts, knowing everyone in the room was looking to her for leadership at this very moment, Jensen Maddox included, though he would never admit it. "If we pool our resources, Grandfather, we have the best chance of getting to the bottom of this investigation sooner rather than later."

He swung his head in her direction, an obstinate expression riding the hard angles of his face. "Why would I trust the security team of a Calcagni?" He thumbed a hand rudely in Rhys's direction. "Might I remind you that—"

"Because we have a common enemy," she cut in. "We need each other. All emotions aside, it's just smart business."

He slapped his hands on the arms of his chair and pushed to his feet. "This!" He circled his finger in the air to take in the occupants of the room. "Looks like a heck of a lot more than business. And you, granddaughter," he stabbed the air in her direction, "are the one I'll be holding accountable for the fallout when this is over."

He leaned over her chair and jutted his chin, still shaking his finger. "I made you, Alora Maddox, and I just as easily can un-make you. I chose you from a lineup of motherless infants. I gave you your name and every penny you own. I poured my life experience into you, grooming you for the very title you now hold. Everything you are and ever will be, you owe to me." He stabbed his finger against his chest and dragged in a labored breath. "If you ever give me reason to withdraw my support, you will return to being nothing."

His face red with fury, Jensen Maddox straightened and dropped his shaking hand to his side.

As she absorbed his torrent of threats, Alora felt as if all the light, joy, and color in the world was being drained right out of the room. It left her insides cold and her heart aching for everyone who'd had the misfortune to overhear her grandfather's words. She didn't dare look at her siblings, unable to imagine the amount of hurt they were absorbing. She didn't dare look at anyone else, either, unable to bear the pity they must be feeling for her.

It was all she could do to swallow the crushing pain of rejection. Good heavens! She and her grandfather had never been close. And she'd certainly spent her fair share of her teenage years wishing he was warmer and more affectionate, but she'd always assumed he still loved her in his own way — that he merely wasn't one of those people who was good at showing it. His words, however, made her wonder if he had any capacity for love at all.

It was now painfully clear that her value to him

did not extend beyond the boardroom. To him, she'd never been anything more than a pawn to move around on a chessboard. No wonder he'd been so easily fooled by Kellan's twin. Apparently, he didn't harbor any genuine affection for any of his grand-children.

All self-pity aside, nothing that had transpired in Jacey and Luca's dining room this evening altered the fact that Alora's actions would continue to affect those she loved the most. They were waiting on her next move right now. Her next words. Her guidance.

She rose from her seat and smoothed her hands down the skirts of her borrowed party dress. Her heart might be numb, but her problem-solving skills were very much still intact. "As soon as you provide me with the name of your adoption company, Grandfather, and any other information you think might be useful in our investigation, I'm going to use it to personally ensure that those trying to harm our family are brought to justice."

Her grandfather's choleric expression settled back into its habitual hard, assessing lines. "I'll have my secretary forward every document I have on file concerning your brother's adoption."

"Tonight, if possible," she returned crisply. "I'm not going to rest until this is over."

A hint of grudging approval stole across his features. He gave her a sharp nod. "For what it's worth, I don't think Kellan's twin is capable of pulling off something of this magnitude."

She trained an unblinking stare on him. "Meaning what, exactly?"

"He's too damaged." He slapped at the air. "I've had half a dozen specialists examine him. According to their prognosis, we seem to be looking at some form of a Dissociative Identity Disorder."

"As in a split personality?" Her brows rose in shocked contemplation.

"Among other things. He was in a fetal position when I left him earlier, babbling at the wall like a small child."

"You left him alone with Grandmother?" she inquired sharply.

"Of course not!" He scowled. "We hired a full-time nurse weeks ago."

"Good. Keep him under her care and out of the spotlight." She narrowed her gaze at her grandfather, suddenly realizing what it would take to buy his compliance. "DRAW Corporation stock shares can't afford to have another PR nightmare hit the fan right now."

"Agreed." He spoke between clenched teeth.

"Go ahead and forward me his medical reports, as well. I have some ideas about how we might use his condition to generate some positive PR for our firm."

Jensen Maddox's chuckle was as scratchy as sandpaper. "Now we're talking."

"Kellan can handle that for us. The *real* Kellan." He had a gift for managing PR-related issues. She pasted on a smile she didn't feel. "As for the investigation into his twin, I'll notify you once I've gathered the proof we need to make an indictment."

He snorted. "It won't be him you'll be indicting. Mark my words. No court will put him behind bars. A padded cell maybe..."

His words made Alora's mind race over a new set of possibilities as she walked him to the front entrance of Luca and Jacey's home. Kellan's twin might not be capable of harming their family on his own, but what if someone was using him to do exactly that? But who? And why?

"I would appreciate your discretion on the location of my temporary office." She forced herself to meet her grandfather's gaze and steadily hold it, knowing he respected a show of strength above all else. "Be assured I have my own security team in place."

He inclined his head a fraction. "I cannot say I like the idea of you working here, but so long as it doesn't keep you from fulfilling your responsibilities, I'll overlook it for now." With that, he made his exit.

Alora watched him through the glass doors as his chauffeur, who'd likely kept her grandfather's limousine idling throughout his short visit, jogged around to open his door. After they drove away, she tipped her head back for a moment to let out a long, pent-up sigh. She stared at the tall, domed foyer ceiling, unable to summon the heart to return to the dining room just yet. There were those who would be disappointed at her sudden exodus, but they would understand her reasons for wanting to be alone right now.

A pair of strong arms encircled her middle, and Rhys's scent and strength enveloped her. His rich baritone rumbled low in her ear. "No one can ever take credit for the miracle that is Alora Maddox. You were fearfully and wonderfully made by our Creator, and I am humbly grateful to have someone as incredible as you in my life."

Silent sobs shook her at his words, pouring through her and washing away the pain of a thousand unloving moments spent in the presence of her adoptive parents and grandparents. She gripped his steely forearms and held on to the precious gift he was offering her — himself.

It was several gasping moments before the storm in her subsided. Then she gently twisted in his embrace to face him. "I know I probably look like a wreck right now, but don't you dare pity me, Rhys Calcagni."

"I don't." He held her gaze, drinking her in with his beautiful, bourbon-hued eyes. "I admire you, love. The way you handled yourself this evening." He gave a long, low whistle. "Most other people I know would have started swinging, but not you. You never lost sight of what was at stake for everyone in the room. If anything, I respect you more after what happened back there, not less."

"Good, because know this. I wouldn't wish any of it away, even if I could. Not my humble beginnings or my adopted name. Not my callous grandfather or his heartless ambitions. Not even my car accident. Every step of my disjointed journey has brought me to where I am now. To you," she finished brokenly.

The kiss they shared this time was frantic, bordering on desperation. Alora's grandfather had made it deathly clear the risks she was taking by allying herself with the Calcagnis. Her position in her family and in their firm was on the line. The cost for moving forward with her marriage to Rhys was going to be steep, indeed.

Rhys broke off the kiss first, palming her cheek to rub his thumb across her lower lip. "As much as I hate to say this, it's time to get back to work, chief."

Appreciating him for understanding that she couldn't afford to take the evening off, she smiled through her tears. "I'll have Titus help me comb through every inch of the files my grandfather sends over."

"We're going to get through this together, love."

She adored his constant reminders that she was not alone. "One way or the other," her smile was damp and tremulous, "though I may be job-hunting on the other side of it."

"We'll see about that." His gaze turned flinty. "You're on my team now, love. We'll fight our battles together."

"Speaking of being a team, I would like your help with one project in particular." She traced a finger down the side of his neck, adoring the warm, pulsing brush of skin against skin.

"As usual, you have my undivided attention."

"Thank you." His impassioned declaration made her smile. "I wasn't just trying to unruffle my grandfather's feathers with my comment about using Kellan's twin to generate some positive PR. I knew the way I worded it would stroke his ego, but Kellan's twin is family; and the truth is, he needs our help. I'd like to pitch his medical condition as an R&D project to the Black Tie Billionaires. Many of them already have a huge heart for charity. However, I think your marvelous gift for charts and graphs might stand a chance of going further than my heartfelt sentiments in convincing them that this is the next project they should get behind."

"Aw, only a few hours engaged, and you're already jotting out your first honey-do list," he teased.

"Rhys!" A breathy laugh escaped her.

"Consider it done, love. I'll have some numbers crunched and beautiful charts flowing for you in no time. Anything else?" He waggled his brows at her as he inched her backwards to the stairs leading to her guest room.

"This." She tugged his head down for another kiss.

CHAPTER 12: HOSTILE TAKEOVER

ALORA

R hys returned alone to the dining room, which was fast emptying. Kellan said something about not letting Luca's phenomenal video game room on the lower level go to waste. He proceeded to toss good-natured insults in Greyson's direction until he agreed to join him.

Knox shrugged and followed them from the room. "May as well do my part in fraternizing with the enemy," he announced in a loud whisper as he strode past Rhys.

Rhys bumped the fist his younger brother held up. "Knock yourself out."

Jacey and Bailey were hugging and saying their goodbyes to each other. Rhys paused in the oversized archway, giving them their space for their sisterly moment.

Don approached to shake Rhys's hand. "Let us know if you need anything."

"You know I will." He nodded at Bailey when she glanced over at them.

Her smile was cautiously searching. "Take care of her for us."

He knew she was referring to her oldest sister. "I'm trying to." Though it was getting harder and harder to think and act objectively where Alora was concerned. She was fast becoming his biggest reason for existing. All he could do was pray for the strength and wisdom to make the right choices in the coming days, no matter how difficult they were.

"How is she?" Jacey demanded once she, Luca, and Rhys were left alone in the dining room. She propped her hands on her slender hips and faced him squarely.

"Unshakable." He shoved open his blazer to tuck a hand in the pocket of his trousers as he waited to catch Luca's eye. His oldest brother was standing behind his chair at the head of the table, scrolling through messages on his phone.

"That despicable toad of a man made her cry, didn't he?" she stormed, flipping a hank of long, blonde hair over her shoulder. "Sometimes I just want to put my hands around his hateful neck and squeeze. Grr!" She mimed the act of choking someone.

Rhys smiled. "It's Alora we're talking about.

She'll face her demons in true Alora style and beat them."

Jacey's mouth twisted with distaste. "The demons shouldn't be wearing the faces of one's own family members."

He couldn't agree more, so he kept silent, preferring not to say anything abrasive about her family. The recent truce between the Calcagni and Maddox siblings was delicate at best. He didn't want to do anything to damage it.

"The things he said to her," Jacey shook her head, her blue eyes waxing anxious, "nobody should ever have to listen to stuff like that. I know people called me foolish and impulsive when I walked away from all of it. Correction, I ran away." She made a wry face. "Sure, I harbor a few regrets for some of the stupider things I've done, but leaving behind the hateful Maddox name is not one of them."

Never before had Rhys adored his sister-in-law so much. "You've made a fine addition to the Calcagni clan, sis." He liked her spark and spirit, along with her fierce loyalty to those she loved. More than anything, he appreciated how happy she made his brother. He'd watched Luca for years as he shouldered the pressures of being a CEO in flat-lipped silence.

Though Rhys had his oldest brother's back when it came to all things work-related, there were voids he simply couldn't fill for him. It was a lonely place at the top, but Jacey had made it less lonely for Luca — a lot less lonely. Lord willing, Rhys aspired to do the same for Alora.

"Thanks. I have my moments," Jacey muttered. "Appreciate you listening to me vent."

"No problem." He grinned when, in her usual impulsive style, she danced in his direction to kiss his cheek.

She directed her sparkling gaze at her husband next. "I'm going to the nursery to squeeze hug our son and keep him up past his bedtime. Do you want to join me?"

"Yes." The look they shared was charged with intimacy. "I just need a few minutes with Rhys first."

She made a pouty face at Rhys. "Don't keep him too long, or I'm taking back my kiss."

He pretended to look down his nose at her. "Sorry. No refunds."

She left the room in a swirl of red sequins, silver stilettos, and the scent of exotic flowers.

"You're one very lucky man." Rhys stepped farther into the room, removing his hand from his pocket.

"I am." Luca grimaced at his phone, not the reaction Rhys was expecting to their exchange.

"Bad news?" He rapped his knuckles on the end of the dining room table.

"Yes and no." Luca's expression turned calculating, the way he looked when he was presiding over an especially difficult negotiation. "All day, I've been watching DRAW Corporation stock shares trade, and there's one group in particular that seems to be making a grab for it. Twenty thousand shares at noon and another fifty thousand shares or so right before the close of business."

So it was beginning. Rhys's chest tightened at the knowledge that DRAW Corporation likely wouldn't survive the sharks circling it.

"As to whether we join in the fray, I've decided to make it entirely your call." Luca looked up from his screen. "To be honest, part of me wouldn't mind watching Jensen Maddox bleed. After all he has done to hurt my wife and her sisters." He shook his head. "However, I respect the position you're in. If you say no, we'll back off and never speak of it again. But if you say yes, we'll start buying first thing in the morning. I already have the shell corporations and accounts set up. I guarantee that no one will see us coming." His smile didn't reach his eyes. "Until it's too late to stop us, that is."

"I wish I was at liberty to discuss this with Alora first." It was the most difficult decision Rhys had ever made. However, he understood the laws surrounding insider trading. To legally protect all parties involved, there could be no communication between him and Alora about the proposed buyout. No collaboration of any sort between the executives at the two firms that could be construed afterward as an attempt to artificially move the price of the stock.

"You know you can't. It's proprietary information."

"Did you send them an offer outright?" It was common business practice to attempt to first buy the company via a letter of intent. However, most executive boards stubbornly refused to negotiate, no matter how bad their financials looked. They simply took the purchase letter as a warning shot and battened down their hatches for the coming battle.

"I did, and she rejected it."

Rhys nodded. Alora's response made sense. She would have been following the will of the board, so there was no way of knowing what her true feelings were on the topic of selling her company.

He swiftly weighed their options one last time. Hours ago, he'd worried that buying out DRAW Corporation's stock via a hostile takeover might be construed by Alora as the ultimate betrayal. He inwardly shuddered at the thought she might chalk up their entire romantic relationship as one big grab for power on his part. However, Jensen Maddox's threats had changed the game for him. If the man was genuinely capable of removing his own granddaughter from her position as CEO merely because of her desire to pursue a congenial working relationship with the owners of Genesis & Sons, then what would the man do when he found out she'd gone and married one of them?

Buying out DRAW Corporation suddenly seemed like the only way to save Alora's job.

Rhys's voice came out terse and strained. "What are your thoughts about serving as their holding company and retaining all key personnel?"

Luca's calculating expression remained unchanged. "I can understand your sentiments on the topic, and I'll take them under advisement. The holding company option makes sense, considering they are a well-established brand. I also like the idea of offering to keep Alora at the helm, if she's willing, to ensure the smoothest transition. Not to mention her hefty golden parachute clause would make the transaction highly unprofitable in the near term if we let her go. Everyone else will need to reapply for their jobs and go through our normal screening process. You know the drill. It's the only way to operate a successful company."

"What about Kellan and Greyson?"

"What about them, Rhys?"

"They're your family by marriage now, and they are about to become mine."

"We always take care of family. That won't ever change."

"Then start buying." Rhys felt like the weight of the world was crushing his shoulders. "Buy up every blessed share of DRAW Corporation stock and force them to a vote." Satisfaction surged through him, and no small amount of glee.

A welcome side benefit to saving Alora's position would be watching the mighty Jensen Maddox fall at last. The man had cheated his way to the top, back-stabbing every step of the way and pulling others down in the attempt to make himself look taller. Years ago, he'd betrayed his closest friend, Rhys's grandfather; stolen Edric Calcagni's fiancée on his way out the door; and used their proprietary secrets to build his empire. He deserved to lose.

"Consider it done."

"I'd like to be the one to inform Alora when the time comes."

"Naturally."

"And if our engagement survives the merger, I want you to serve as the best man at our wedding."

"I would be honored." Luca's harsh expression softened. "You know I would."

The time for secrets was over. If Rhys and Luca succeeded in taking ownership of DRAW Corporation, there would be nothing left for anyone to hold over Alora. Nothing to keep her from planning the kind of wedding ceremony most brides dreamed of having.

WITHIN THE HOUR, Alora forwarded the name of the adoption company that had processed all five of her and her siblings' adoptions. It was called Real Sons, LLC. What Titus dug up on the company in the middle of the night was enough to make Rhys's blood run cold.

In the wee hours of the morning, he dialed Luca, who picked up on the third ring. "This better be good, because it just cost you Jacey's kiss."

"The adoption company the Maddox family used was called Real Sons, LLC."

"That sounds fairly innocuous," Lucas mused.

"Until you read about their long and sordid history of complaints and lawsuits."

"Ouch!"

"Ouch is right. They've changed the name of their firm several times since the Maddox adoptions, most likely to mucky the process for those seeking to file claims against them — everything from True Sons, to New Sons, to Rightful Sons."

"At least they were consistent in their branding."

"And equally consistent in blurring the lines of the law, apparently. Allegations against them include baby-napping, bribery, extortion, baby swapping, and child negligence." Rhys was horrified at the knowledge that the woman he loved and wanted to marry had passed through such a shady process. It was a miracle of Biblical proportions that she'd grown into the brilliant, talented, and successful woman she was today. Other infants in the care of Real Sons, LLC hadn't been so lucky.

Luca was silent for a moment. "Any luck on tracing Kellan's twin?"

"Yes. He was born to a wealthy woman who'd undergone extensive infertility treatments that resulted in the conception of triplets."

"Say it isn't so!" Luca groaned. It meant Kellan Maddox had not one, but two, biological siblings.

"Identical triplets, which is rare. For reasons we may never know, she only kept one and adopted out the other two, but that isn't even the most interesting part."

"Do tell all," Luca commanded dryly.

"Her son was involved in a boating accident two years ago and returned home with a traumatic head injury that baffled the medical specialists."

"I really don't like where this is going."

"Me, neither. Her son exhibited Dissociative Identity Disorder symptoms — far from the normal result of a traumatic head injury. Most unfortunately, he was serving as the president of a major subsidiary at the time. Their stock price plummeted at the news of instability among their senior leadership, and they were subsequently acquired via a hostile takeover."

"Meaning Real Sons swapped out what's-his-name with the split personality for the triplet who was serving as president." Luca sounded incensed.

"Yes. We believe his name was Maximus. He was fired, by the way, the moment the merger went through. Sadly, his remains washed up on the river's edge a few months later."

"The company president's remains, I presume?" That meant they could add homicide to Real Son's list of crimes. Which meant Kellan Maddox wasn't likely meant to survive his boating accident. It was a miracle he was alive — the loose thread they would use to topple this heinous ring of criminals.

"I can only assume, since the other Maximus is still with us."

"So instead of the villain of our story, Maximus is actually one of the victims."

"Looks like. Alora was right to try to help him." Rhys shook his head. Her capacity for compassion, despite her own recent brush with death, truly amazed him. "She asked me to help her craft a pitch to the Black Tie Billionaires to search for a cure for Maximus's medical condition. To date, he doesn't fit any known diagnosis." The Black Tie Billionaires were an elite group of philanthropists who took on some of the world's most unique social outreach and charity projects. The trick was getting their attention and convincing them why your project should receive priority over their long list of applicants.

He planned to give them just enough informa-tion about Kellan and his imposter brother to pique their interest — triplets separated at birth, one with a disorder that an unscrupulous firm had exploited to perform massive amounts of financial fraud.

"Alright, well, let me get back to trying to stay married. We've got a big day ahead of us tomorrow." Humor infused Luca's voice. It was followed by a sleepy-sounding female murmur.

"Right." Sleep. It was the last thing on Rhys's mind. "Just so you know, I'll have to step away for about an hour tomorrow afternoon. Alora and I are going to pay a visit to city hall, so we can turn in the application for our wedding license." His brothers would have to carry on with the buyout in his absence, keeping the momentum of the takeover moving forward.

"Congratulations!" Luca sounded more awake this time. "I didn't realize things had progressed to the point of setting a date. I'm happy to hear it."

An excited squeal sounded in the background, as Jacey perceived something monumental had taken place.

Rhys was grinning when he disconnected the line. He showered and forced himself to get horizontal afterward, but he mostly stared at the ceiling the rest of the night. There was so much bad mixed in with the good these days. So much sorrow mixed with the joy. So many new questions, but so few answers.

◌

THE FOLLOWING MORNING, Rhys bounded out of bed with a burst of restless energy. He donned a suit and grabbed a ham and egg croissant on the run to the irritation of Heston, who would have preferred to see his employer adjourn to the breakfast room for a proper repast.

He arrived to Genesis & Sons at the crack of seven. It was a stalwart old office building, made of white and gray stone, overlooking the inlet waters. For decades, it had withstood the fury of snow, rain, hail, and a few mild earthquakes like a sturdy fortress. Several times, the Calcagnis had debated the idea of building a new office or relocating to a more modern structure to keep up with the times; but they had always ended up renovating, instead. Rhys wouldn't change a thing about the building if he could.

The walls were paneled with rich mahogany, and the tile floor on the main level displayed an intricate mosaic design. One of Rhys's favorite features in the building, however, was the antique clock displayed behind the receptionist's booth. Custom designed by a Black Hills clockmaker from Germany, its copper gears and chains were affixed to the wall, comprising the largest clock in all of Anchorage. It had been featured in magazines around the world.

Rhys rode the *authorized personnel only* elevator to the top floor of the high-rise and was unsurprised to discover Luca was already in his office. He waved a WiFi headset at his younger brother.

Rhys took it, fit it around his ear, and adjusted the mouthpiece. When the market opened, he and his brothers were going to be placing high volumes of stock trades in a short period of time via multiple accounts.

Knox joined them a few minutes later and pulled on a third headset. "You two look like you're heading to a funeral," he noted with a cocky grin. "Am I truly the only one in the room looking forward to destroying our biggest rival? This has been a long time coming!" He removed his eggplant hued blazer, tossed it over the back of one of Luca's conference chairs, and rubbed his hands together gleefully.

He came to stand between his brothers in front of the wall of glass overlooking the gulf. Stuffing his hands in his pockets, he gave a huff of supreme satisfaction.

"A few months ago I might have enjoyed it more," Rhys conceded.

"Does your change of heart have something to do with a certain red-head?" his younger brother teased.

"Something like that." Rhys turned away from the glass to eye the screens on the wall that were flashing with pre-trading news. It appeared the market was going to open down several points. That would only work to their benefit.

"Are you ready for this?" Luca moved past him to his desk in the center of the room.

"As ready as I'm going to be." Rhys would have preferred to go on vacation and come back when it was all over.

"We're doing it for all the right reasons," Luca reminded. "If you play your cards right, your bride might actually consider it to be a wedding gift."

"A what?" Knox looked astounded. He elbowed his brother none too gently. "Look at you! My steady older brother taking a walk on the wild side."

Rhys nodded, though his thoughts turned glum. His bride *might* consider the buyout a wedding gift. She might also consider it the ultimate betrayal. He kept his eye on the scrolling headlines at the bottom of the screen. A news blip about DRAW Corporation appeared.

More trouble on the horizon for DRAW Corporation, as authorities determine the recent explosion at top executive Greyson Maddox's estate was the result of arson.

As expected, the news did DRAW Corporation no favors. Their stock share price opened down — way down — and the Calcagni brothers started buying.

CHAPTER 13: EMERGENCY VOTE

ALORA

Alora arrived at city hall with Titus Rand a few minutes early and was a little surprised that Rhys was not already there. He'd always struck her as being a very punctual kind of guy. Worried that he'd gotten caught in traffic, she glanced up at the clock tower on the beige stucco and stone building. She only had about an hour of time to spare, so she hoped he showed up soon.

It was a beautiful spring afternoon with plenty of sunshine. She was glad she'd worn both sunglasses and a wide hat. That way she could protect her privacy as well as her complexion. She took advantage of the gorgeous weather to hold down a park bench and scroll through her messages while Titus patrolled the courtyard. An email was waiting for her from Shep, titled *Open Right Away!*

So she did. It read,

Harold Pezel is favorable toward reopening nego-tiations with DRAW. He is happy to hear you are recovering from your car accident and looks forward to setting up a conference call.

Alora tipped her face up to the sun and whispered a prayer of gratitude. *I'm back!* It felt good to have something go right, for once. The executives at Pezel seemed to have no idea that the real reason for the delay in their negotiations was because DRAW Corporation was the target of a major financial fraud scheme. As bad as things looked for her company right now, they would be a lot worse if word got out about the attempted takeover. Their stock share prices had taken a steep hit in recent days, but a contract with a solid company like Pezel would go a long way toward putting them back on track.

I can do this. No, it was more than that. *I have to do this.* Greyson, Kellan, and Bailey were depending on her to set a corporate agenda that would bolster revenues and guide them out of their current slump.

Her siblings had been a little alarmed about the buyout letter they'd received from an unknown company called G&S, Inc. Her team of attorneys had assured her it was nothing more than a start-up. Probably some fresh college grads trolling the stock market for low hanging fruit. Regardless of who they were, she had a golden parachute clause — thanks to her grandfather while he'd served as CEO — that would require any acquiring company to pay her an extravagant severance package if they let her go. It was common practice for small companies like hers to protect themselves with agreements like these. She only wished that all the key executives at DRAW had the same protection. It was something she intended to bring to the board's attention at their next meeting.

"Hello, beautiful!" Rhys's shadow blanketed her as he leaned in from behind her park bench to press a kiss to her cheek.

"Rhys!" she hissed, touching her cheek. Although he was wearing a hat and tinted sunglasses, it wouldn't take a rocket scientist to identify them if anyone was paying close enough attention.

"There's no paparazzi in the area. Titus checked," he assured, walking around the park bench with a grin. "Come with me, love. The marriage license clerk awaits us."

She accepted his outstretched hand and used it to pull herself to her feet.

Titus nodded at her from a discreet distance and made his way to the front arched entranceway. He positioned himself by the iron railing and waited for them to approach.

"Did you bring any additional paperwork for me to sign?" He arched an inquiring brow at her.

"No." She felt the start of a blush warming her cheeks. "If you're not going to ask me to sign a prenuptial agreement, I see no reason to ask you to sign one, either. Your net worth far exceeds mine — at least at the moment." She made a face. "The market hasn't been very kind to our stock prices lately."

"You'll weather the storm." He squeezed her fingers. "You always do."

"Thank you for your vote of confidence." They walked hand-in-hand up the sidewalk, beneath the lovely arched windows, and stepped inside the city hall building. "I appreciate all your support the past several weeks, Rhys. I know I probably look like I'm floundering, but things are looking up."

"How so?" he asked cheerfully.

She was excited to be able to tell someone who would both understand and care. "An opportunity to engage in a very warm negotiation. A bit of a blast from the past — someone who wasn't scared away by our many executive level misfortunes."

"I'm happy to hear it." He raised her hand to his lips and pressed a kiss to her fingers. Then he let her hand go, so they could pass through a metal detector.

As they approached the city clerk windows, Alora removed the precious license application from her briefcase. "I spilled a few drops of my morning tea on it, so it's been properly christened." She chuckled. "Plus, it smells amazing." She selected the window on the far end of the customer service counter for two reasons — it offered them a bit of privacy, plus the clerk was an elderly woman who looked half asleep. With a little luck, she wouldn't recognize them or their names.

"You smell pretty amazing, yourself." Rhys stepped close enough for her to feel his body heat through her navy dress suit. He rested a hand on her waistline as they waited for the clerk to process their application.

As Alora had hoped, the expression of the clerk didn't change when she read their application. She made a few notes, recorded something on her computer screen, then passed it back through the opening beneath the window.

"I'll need both of you to sign it while I witness your signatures," she informed them in a matter-of-fact voice.

Rhys's cheek brushed Alora's as he reached around her to sign his name with a strong, confident flourish.

She caught her breath. *It's done. I've applied to marry a Calcagni.* All hell was going to break loose in the Maddox realm when her family found out. And they would. She had no idea why she ever thought she was going to be able to keep their marriage a secret. It was only a matter of time before the news leaked out.

"You okay, love?" Rhys's low, rich baritone caressed her ear.

She nodded, catching her lower lip between her teeth. It just felt like too much was happening too quickly. Her heart was in such a tangle of emotions that she longed for... Alora blinked a few times when she realized she was wishing for a mother to confide in, all of a sudden. Unfortunately, she and Nora Maddox had never been close. Her adoptive mother had always been married to her job. She was as grasping and ambitious as her father-in-law, more image-conscious than people-conscious.

"Are you sure you're okay?" Rhys's voice adopted an anxious note.

"Just a little overwhelmed," she confessed in a breathy voice, watching the clerk stamp their application and write out her signature as a witness.

"That's understandable. You're about to be a bride." There was a smile in his voice as he nuzzled her earlobe. "Mine."

His. It was one small word, but it packed so much meaning. "It's such a big step," she whispered.

"We'll take it together, love," he whispered back.

They left the city hall building hand-in-hand, and Rhys followed her to her SUV. He opened the passenger door for her, while Titus hopped in the driver's seat. "Do you have any plans for dinner tonight?"

"Other than joining Jacey and Luca in their spectacular dining room again? No."

"Perfect. I was hoping you would join me at my hillside hacienda for one of Chef Heston's masterpieces."

"It's a date!" She beamed up at him.

"Good." He pulled her away from the open door of her vehicle so he could enjoy some modicum of privacy as he tenderly kissed her. "I'll have Major come pick you up at six, if that sounds alright with your schedule."

"You're the best."

To her surprise, his smile slipped. "There's nothing I wouldn't do for you, love. You know that, right?"

"Why, Rhys!" She reached up to touch his cheek. "I guess I'm not the only one feeling a little overwhelmed by what we just did."

"It's not that." He curled his fingers around hers and held her hand captive against the side of his face. "If anything, I wish we were already married, so I could quit worrying about something happening to make you change your mind."

She sniffed. "Then apparently grooms get to experience attacks of the ol' nerves the same as we brides do, because I cannot imagine any scenario that would change my mind about marrying you. I mean that, Rhys!"

"I wish my own imagination wasn't so active, then," he groaned in a low voice.

She leaned in his direction to kiss his nose. "In three days, I'm going to marry you, Rhys Calcagni, come rain or shine. I give you my word. Though my stock shares might not be worth much at the moment, my word is."

His smile was sad. "No doubt we will have our ups and downs as a couple. A few spats, even."

"No doubt." She stood on her tiptoes to kiss his nose again.

"No matter what arises in the way of family drama or corporate rivalries in the coming days, please know that I love you, Alora."

She was taken aback by the anxious tenor of his voice. "I do, Rhys. In fact, it's one of the few things in the world I've never had any reason to doubt."

"Good." He kissed her lingeringly. "Ah, there's one more thing I wanted to discuss with you." He pulled a small, black velvet box from the pocket of his trousers and popped open the lid. Inside was a stunning, round pink diamond in a gold setting. It had to be as large as four or five carats. A delicate gold chain was threaded through it.

"Rhys!" she gasped. "It's lovely!" This must be the family heirloom he'd mentioned giving her.

"So are you. May I put it on you?"

She nodded, speechless with happiness.

"I'm assuming around your neck is the safest place for it right now." He clasped the chain behind her nape and claimed her mouth again in a way that left her weak and breathless.

"See you at 6:oo?" he muttered against her lips.

"See you at 6:oo," she promised softly.

Titus stared straight ahead as he drove them out of the garage. This surprised Alora. Normally he was more talkative.

"Is it just me, or did Rhys seem a little nervous back there?" she inquired in a wistful voice.

Titus probably thought she was crazy asking him something so personal, but he could suck it up in silence, because she had no one else to confide in.

"He worries about you all the time. That's all." Titus still didn't smile or look in her direction. He drove with one arm on the wheel, since his other arm remained in a sling.

"I've just never seen him so tense," she muttered, half to herself.

"If your roles were reversed, you'd feel the same way," Titus declared. "Think about it, Alora. He's had to watch you suffer in ways no man should ever have to watch the woman he loves suffer."

She was silent for a moment. "So you don't think he's having second thoughts about marrying me?"

"You're kidding, right?" Titus exploded, glancing her way at last. "That man loves you more than life, itself. He would probably lose his mind if anything else bad happened to you. Shoot!" He made a scoffing sound. "Maybe this would be a good time to let you in on a little secret he's been keeping from you. I don't mind telling you now that you're going to marry the guy."

"Oh?" She felt a little dazed. If Titus was spilling secrets, what was the world coming to?

"I own a security firm called Rand Industries. We used to hire ourselves out for gigs all over the northwest; but that changed when Rhys Calcagni hired my entire staff for the sole purpose of keeping you safe. He had the medical center literally crawling with muscle the whole time you were in your coma."

She pressed both hands to her chest. "So you're not simply one of his many bodyguards?" Way down deep inside, she'd suspected he was more, but...

"Rhys Calcagni only has one bodyguard, princess, if you can even call him that. He also serves as his driver and co-pilot, among other things."

"You mean Major?"

"Yep. Major is his go-to guy. The rest of us were hired because of you."

"I'm...wow!" What Rhys had done for her took her breath away.

"You can say that again." He made a face at her. "So now you know why I put up with your skinny little troublesome self in stilettos. It's job security, ma'am!"

She wrinkled her forehead at him. "I could have you fired for insubordination."

"You could certainly try," Titus chuckled.

She shot him a teasing glance. "I might reconsider keeping you on our payroll after we're married, if you swallow your pride long enough to ask that pretty ICU nurse out to dinner."

"Who says I haven't already?" he shot back.

"Oh, my goodness, Titus!" She clapped her hands in delight. "Did you really?"

"No." His smile disappeared.

"Okay, you're officially on probation, mister," she scolded.

"Duly noted, princess." He drove her past the front of the white, chrome, and glass DRAW Corporation high-rise to the parking garage entrance.

Her phone was buzzing with incoming messages their entire elevator ride up to her office.

Shep Peterson was waiting for her right outside the elevator. "Thank God you're here!" His dark gaze was frantic.

"What is going on?" She started to brush past him, but he moved to stand in front of her.

"I'm sorry, Miss Maddox, but I was asked to escort you to the board room the moment you stepped inside the building."

"Why? Is there a fire?" She wished he would return to his desk and quit acting so dramatic. She was anxious to get back to work on the Pezel account.

"You could call it that. We're being bought out."

"What!" He had her attention now.

"Your grandfather thinks it's that company called G&S who sent us the lowball offer a few days ago."

"What else do you know?" Panic gripped her.

This can't be happening. She'd just applied for a marriage certificate. It was supposed to be a happy day. A time for celebrating. She had a dinner date with Rhys in two hours, for crying out loud!

"Mr. Maddox has his attorneys combing through everything they can get their hands on, which isn't much. Looks like G&S used a set of shell companies to hide behind. All-in-all, it was a pretty well-coordinated effort."

She rolled her eyes. "I assume these are the same attorneys who swore a few days ago that we had nothing to worry about?"

He nodded, looking pale.

"Fresh college grads, my hide!" she spat, though she knew there was no point in Monday-morning quarterbacking the buyout attempt. It had happened on her watch, so it was more her fault than anyone else's. She should have never trusted her grandfather's advice. He was getting up there in years and had been too distracted lately by Kellan's imposter's antics.

"I don't think they're fresh out of college any more than you do, ma'am," Shep assured.

"What percentage did they grab?" she demanded, tossing her briefcase on the nearest work table.

"Nearly all of it."

Her mind ran feverishly over the details. "Well, even if they managed to buy all of our common stock, that would still only leave them with forty-nine percent." Her family had been careful to keep the majority shares in-house. Each of them owned a piece of it. So if the new owners of their common stock forced the board to hold a vote for a change in leadership, they would lose.

"That's assuming your family will be unified in their vote," Shep reminded in a cautious voice. He winced when she looked his way.

His words slowly sank in, and she felt the color leave her face. He was right. Jacey and Bailey owned shares, neither of whom were directly employed by DRAW Corporation any longer. And their grandfather's meltdown in Jacey's dining room the other evening likely had not gained back one ounce of her floundering loyalty. Quite the opposite. His actions would have only solidified Jacey's devotion to Luca, CEO of Genesis & Sons — the biggest rival of DRAW Corporation.

"G&S," she whispered in horror, as the truth of their identity sank in. G&S was Genesis & Sons. It *had* to be! Rhys and his brothers had bought out her company. The breath slowly seeped out of her. "I need to sit down," she gasped.

Shep managed to drag a chair out from beneath her conference table just in time. She sank into it, feeling close to passing out.

This meant that Rhys had known about the buyout attempt the entire time they were together today. He'd known it when he applied for a license to marry her. He'd known it when he held her and kissed her. He'd known it when he was acting all wonky about...*oh, dear Heavens!* He'd known it when he was flipping out at the possibility of her changing her mind about marrying him. Her breath came out in a shudder.

Oh, Rhys! What have you done?

She didn't realize her eyes were closed until someone pressed a mug of coffee in her hands. Her eyelids flew open.

Titus was standing there, looking singularly concerned but not surprised.

"You knew about this?" she whispered.

He didn't respond.

Tears spilled down her cheeks, soaking the collar of her lacy white shirt. "Why?" she cried. "Just tell me why!"

He shook his head and crouched down in front of her. "Alora, all I can tell you is that man would lay down on a set of tracks and allow a train to run over him, if that's what it took to protect you."

"That's your line?" Her voice rose to a shrill note. "You're saying he did this to protect me?"

"It's the only reason I can come up with."

"Unfortunately, there was no one to protect me from him!" Full of bitterness, she cupped the steaming mug of coffee between shaking hands. Her throat was too tight to attempt a sip, but she craved its warmth. *How could I have been such a fool?*

It all made sense now — the way Rhys Calcagni had come into her life, seemingly out of nowhere. He'd swept her off her feet, kissed her senseless, given her a false sense of security, and had almost talked her into a marriage without prenuptial agreements. That would have left her stock ownership completely exposed. In a divorce, he would be entitled to fifty percent of her shares, hence the majority vote on all matters concerning DRAW Corporation.

"Shep!" Her voice was sharp, but she was still too dazed for her eyes to focus.

"Yes, ma'am?"

"Let the board know I'm running a few minutes late."

"But—"

"Now, Shep!" She was still in charge, at least for a few more minutes.

By the opening and closing of the door to her suite, she perceived he had followed her order.

"Titus?"

"Still here." His voice was directly in front of her.

"Drive me to Genesis & Sons. I want to meet with Rhys directly. I want him to look me in the face while he explains why he did what he did." Even if what he had to tell her finished breaking her, she deserved the truth. No more secrets. No more hiding behind shell corporations.

"I believe he and his brothers are already on their way here."

"My grandfather will never let them in the building."

"You're the CEO," he reminded gently. "It's your call, not his."

"You're right. Bring him up to my office when he arrives. I don't care where you put Luca and Knox. I'm only interested in meeting with Rhys — alone!"

CHAPTER 14: A HOUSE DIVIDED

RHYS

R hys stared blindly out the window of Luca's black limousine as they cruised the city streets in the direction of DRAW Corporation. He, his brothers, and Jacey were traveling with an extensive entourage to include three attorneys, eight security guards, and two executive assistants. Bailey and Don were traveling in the limousine behind them with their own bevy of attorneys and bodyguards. News helicopters buzzed overhead. It certainly hadn't taken long for word to leak to the paparazzi about the hostile takeover.

It was big, provocative news, too. DRAW Corporation and Genesis & Sons had been major rivals for more than two decades. Their family feud had provided endless fodder to the gossip rags. The buyout would be viewed as a major grab for power —

a mighty corporation swooping in to wield the fatal blow to a wounded adversary.

Rhys could shoulder the rumors and take the gossip in stride. What he couldn't do was bear the thought of losing Alora over it. If she broke their engagement, his last chance at happiness would be forfeited. He wracked his brain for how he and his brothers could have handled the situation differently and came up with nothing. DRAW Corporation was too undervalued. They would have been bought out, one way or the other. It was only a matter of which company would now own them, and he couldn't risk leaving the woman he loved exposed like that.

"We did the right thing," Luca said quietly.

Rhys swiveled his head to catch his brother's eye, knowing the comment was directed at him. What Luca didn't understand — or maybe he did — was that being right wouldn't amount to anything if the buyout cost Rhys his relationship with Alora.

Instead of answering, Rhys watched his brother as drearily as a prisoner on death row awaiting execution. He envied Luca's unshakable calm as he sat in the center of his plush leather seat with one ankle crossed over his knee and an arm slung around his wife's shoulders. He'd never more embodied the image of a CEO — all slicked back and deadly in his dark suit and thick armor of confidence.

Jacey looked far less comfortable about what was about to take place. Despite her obvious discomfort, however, she still managed to look her usual stunning self in a silver-sequenced dress and crystal platform shoes — every inch the pop singing sensation the world knew as J.C. Crew. "I tried to leave the country and come back when this is all over," she offered with a wry smile. "But Luca played one of his CEO cards and vetoed the suggestion."

Knox raised his brows at her. "Since when would a little thing like that stop you?"

"Since he hid my passport." She made a pouty face at her husband.

He bent his head to claim her sass in a searing kiss.

"Now my eyes are bleeding," Knox groaned, pretending to claw at his face.

Rhys twisted his head to stare out the window again, knowing the paparazzi would not likely be kind to Luca in the headlines. He would be criticized for parading his trophy wife through the doors of DRAW Corporation. However, Rhys knew better. Luca was every bit as much in love with his wife as Rhys was in love with her oldest sister. It was the curse at the heart of the feud between their families. Calcagni men had been attracted to Maddox women for three generations and counting.

Rhys was not surprised by the throng of newscasters gathered at the front entrance of DRAW Corporation when they arrived. There were uniformed guards, as well. Rhys braced himself for a hostile clash, wondering if the nightmare could get any worse. However, the guards made no attempt to keep the Calcagnis from entering the building. On the contrary, it soon became apparent that they were helping hold the reporters at bay, so that a path could be cleared for the Calcagnis to reach the front entrance.

"This is too easy," Knox muttered darkly, as he and his brothers strode through the flashing camera bulbs, across DRAW's vast white stucco portico. "Does this mean they'll be waiting for us with machine guns on the other side of the doors?"

"No," Luca said firmly. "This means Alora Maddox is not going to try to stop the vote."

Titus Rand joined them as they stepped through the revolving glass doors. "I've been asked to escort Mr. Rhys Calcagni to a private meeting with Miss Alora Maddox, prior to the vote commencing."

At Luca's raised brows, he affirmed, "Alone."

Luca nodded at Rhys. "Looks like you're going to get your wish."

He was referring to Rhys's request to be the one to explain their actions to Alora. "Well, it was nice knowing you," he muttered in a weak attempt at humor.

No one in their group smiled.

Jacey flew up to him to throw her arms around him. "Go easy on her, will you? This is just as hard for her as it is for you."

He nodded and hugged her back.

Titus led him to a private elevator. It was encased in glass on one side, giving them a view of the cityscape on their way to the top floor.

"How is she?" Rhys demanded hoarsely.

"I don't think she saw this coming, but she's a survivor."

It was killing Rhys to know that he was responsible for all the angst she'd been forced to endure today. "God, give me strength," he muttered.

"And wisdom." Titus spoke something in a language Rhys didn't understand, though it sounded like some sort of Middle Eastern dialect.

"What did you say?" He wrinkled his brow at his head of security.

"'For by wise guidance you can wage your war.' It's from the Book of Proverbs."

"I have no interest in going to battle with Alora." None whatsoever. If she wished to exact any sort of vengeance through him, he would hand her a knife.

Titus grunted. "I told her as much about an hour ago."

Rhys nodded, though he was unable to draw any comfort from Titus's words. All he wanted to do was lay eyes on Alora and see for himself that she was going to be alright...eventually.

The elevator door opened, and Rhys stepped into an elegant waiting area. It was empty of occupants, but a crystal chandelier was suspended over a trio of white leather sofas forming a lounge area. They were clustered around a low, glass-topped table. White roses cascaded from a single blood-red vase in the center of it.

"Stay here. I'll let her know you've arrived." Titus ducked from the sun-drenched room and disappeared down a hall.

The minutes stretched on for an eternity as Rhys waited. He stepped across the room to the floor-to-ceiling window on the far wall and propped his hand against the frame. Bowing his head, he silently prayed for direction.

He and Alora had confessed a dozen or more times to each other that pursuing their attraction wasn't going to be easy. However, he'd never expected it to be quite this hard. He'd pictured himself serving as her debonair secret admirer, indefinitely operating from the shadows, a man of mystery and romance. He's also imagined marrying her in secret and becoming her loving husband behind the scenes. Unfortunately, secrecy wasn't written in the stars for people like them.

There were so few billionaires in the world that they were constantly in the spotlight, constantly under scrutiny, constantly being photographed and gossiped about. In reality, there was no place for him to hide. There never had been. He'd been a fool to believe anything other than the fact his relationship with Alora Maddox had been doomed from the start.

"Rhys!"

He opened his eyes at the sound of her voice, but his head remained bowed and his hand on the window frame. Something hot and wet rolled down his cheek and splashed on the toe of his black leather wingtip, as he realized it might be his last opportunity to share with her what was on his heart.

"I love you, Alora. So much." His voice was rough with emotion. He'd thought of twenty other ways to begin their conversation on the ride up in the elevator, but those were the only words that came to mind now that he was in her presence.

After a long pause, she answered brokenly, "I know." There was another long pause. "I love you, too, Rhys."

His head came up, and he spun around to face her. "You do?"

"Yes." Her face was as damp as his felt, her lovely sea-blue eyes swollen and red-rimmed. "I think I experienced every possible negative emotion in the past hour. Shock, illness, complete mental exhaustion, and a sense of betrayal that cut so deep I thought I was going to shatter."

Each declaration sank into his chest like an ice pick, since he knew he was the sole cause of her suffering. "I would do anything to make this right." He lifted both his hands to run them through his hair and left them there, clutching his head.

A mirthless laugh escaped her. "Isn't that what you've already done?"

He blinked damply at her, not comprehending.

"In the past hour, I also experienced just about every positive emotion known to mankind — gratitude, profound hope, and a love so strong I thought I might actually dissolve from happiness." She drew a shaky breath. "Once I got over the shock of knowing my company had been bought out by yours, I tried to put myself in your shoes and see things from your perspective. And all I could see was a man who had declared his undying love and asked me to marry him with no strings attached, making him as vulnerable as me."

She pressed her hands to her chest, which was when he noticed she was wearing her engagement ring. The pink diamond flashed at him in the evening sun pouring through the window.

He stared at her a moment longer, breathing through the wild bursts of joy cascading over him. "Alora!" He wasn't sure who moved first, only that they flew across the room and landed in each other's embrace.

He hungrily covered her mouth with his, drinking in her sweet trust and loyalty that he knew he fell way short of deserving. "No more secrets," he growled between kisses.

"No more secrets," she agreed, winding her arms around his neck and kissing him back.

It was a long time before Rhys raised his head. "I wanted so badly to tell you about the buyout."

"You couldn't." She shook her head at him. "It was proprietary knowledge."

"Thank you for understanding."

"I'm a CEO." She treated him to a wry smile. "Or was."

"You still are." He was happy to finally be able to tell her that bit of news, as well. "Luca said to consider it a wedding gift. Everyone else will need to reapply for their positions, of course."

Her eyelashes fluttered against her cheeks. "I feel so badly for Greyson and Kellan."

"Don't," he assured tenderly, swooping in to nip soft little kisses on her nose, eyelids, and cheeks. "They're family — twice over, once you marry me — and Calcagni men always take care of family."

"I love being loved by a Calcagni man," she confessed with a sigh. "Nothing has ever made me happier."

He kissed her again. That was the only response that made sense to such an adoring declaration. "Please know the buyout was neither a casual nor an easy decision on our part. We'd been watching the sharks circle you for days before we made our move. If your stock had shown any chances of recovering soon enough to avoid this..." He shook his head, willing her to understand what he was trying to say.

"Believe me, my mind conjured up every

scenario once I recovered enough from my shock to form coherent thoughts again," Alora cupped his cheek, "so there's no need to keep torturing yourself like this. Once I put all the pieces together, I could come up with only one explanation." She smiled tenderly at him. "When I was lying in the coma, you were there holding my hand. It only makes sense that when my company was being destroyed, you would be the one to throw me a lifeline."

"Thank you for seeing it that way, love." His heart pounded at the knowledge he would soon be marrying this beautiful, brilliant woman.

"You're welcome." She beamed at him. "Are you ready to face the dragons with me, now?"

He brushed his mouth against hers one last time. "With you by my side, love, I can face anything."

They walked into the board room with their hands clasped. A collective gasp rose at the sight of them.

Jacey and Bailey's gazes flew to the diamond on Alora's hand and ignited with amazement and joy. Alora's mother sniffed in disdain and tossed her platinum blonde hair over her shoulder, refusing to meet her eye.

Both families were assembled around the lengthy conference table. Jensen Maddox was back at the head of the table, a pointless gesture at this juncture, one that inspired zero respect in Alora. Her grandmother, Iona, was curiously absent. Nora and Pierce

Maddox sat to her grandfather's right. The Maddox and Calcagni siblings were interspersed around the rest of the table. Luca made a point of sitting opposite his wife's grandfather, a clear battle of wills.

With a choleric expression riding his face, Jensen Maddox slammed a gavel down on the table, making several people jump. "I hereby call this meeting—" He paused in irate shock when Titus, who was hovering nearby, snatched the gavel from his hand.

He delivered it across the room to Alora with a flourish. "I believe this rightfully belongs to you, ma'am."

"Thank you, Titus." Squeezing Rhys's fingers one last time, she let go of his hand.

She carried the gavel to the podium at the front of the room, thereby making everyone at the table members of an audience looking up to her. Lightly tapping the gavel on her podium, she announced. "This special meeting of the DRAW Corporation board is called to order."

The room was thick with tension when it came time to place their votes on whether or not Jensen Maddox would get to keep his position.

Alora eyed everyone gravely. "I wish for each individual or entity to state their vote aloud with a yay or a nay when I call their name, without any additional commentary." She drew a deep breath and began. "G&S?"

Luca waved two fingers. "Nay."

Their vote was no surprise to anyone, but it didn't make the bitter expression on her grandfather's face any easier for Alora to bear.

"Jensen Maddox?"

"Yay."

"Iona Maddox?"

"Yay," Jensen Maddox intoned. "Let it be known, I have her proxy vote in hand."

"Nora Maddox?"

"Yay." Her mother's red-painted lips twisted in scorn as she formed the word.

"Pierce Maddox?"

"Yay."

Now came the tough, uncertain votes. "Greyson Maddox?"

"Nay."

Their adoptive mother gasped and half rose out of her chair. "Why, you ungrateful—"

"No additional commentary, please," Alora reminded.

"How dare you!" Nora Maddox stormed. "I'll have you to know—"

Alora nodded at Titus. "Please escort Mrs. Nora Maddox from the room."

When her mother continued to fuss, Alora calmly gave her the option of being escorted out by the police, if she refused to leave with security. The room was much quieter after her mother's exit.

"Alora Maddox votes nay."

"Bailey Maddox?"

Her eyes were downcast. "Nay."

Their grandfather's chin jutted.

"Kellan Maddox?"

"Nay."

This time, Jensen Maddox looked wounded. Once upon a time, he had been closer to Kellan than any other of his grandchildren.

"Jacey Maddox?"

"Nay." She sounded bored.

Alora recorded each vote. "This concludes the vote for Jensen Maddox's position on the board of DRAW Corporation." She turned to him. "You are hereby thanked for your many years of service, sir, and relieved of your position. You will be escorted to your office to collect your belongings."

He made a snarling sound and opened his mouth, as if to begin one of his infamous tirades. Alora motioned for the next two security guards in line to commence with removing him from the room.

Nora Maddox was voted out next; and Pierce Maddox was voted out shortly afterward, although the vote was much closer. Both Kellan and Greyson voted to retain him. The three sisters did not.

During the ensuing hour, Luca, Rhys, and Knox Calcagni, as well as Don Kappelman, were voted in as the newest board members. Several times throughout the tense meeting, Alora met Rhys's gaze. He kissed her with his eyes each time.

After what felt like years, she brought the meeting to a close. "We are adjourned but not dismissed. I have one final matter to announce — make that two, actually — personal matters, not business." She fluttered her left hand at those gathered, so they could get a better look at the winking diamond. "Rhys and I are getting married next week. We will personally deliver your invitations. We hope you can attend."

A round of clapping met her announcement. Luca and Knox both leaped to their feet to clap Rhys on the back and wish him well. Kellan and Greyson remained seated, but both of her brothers looked pleased.

"As for Maximus..." The room stilled at the mention of Kellan's triplet who had tried to impersonate him. "No matter what your feelings are on the topic, he is family, and I think we should do everything in our power to help him get the medical help he needs. My fiancé," she treated Rhys to a warm smile, "has helped me draft a proposal to present to The Black Tie Billionaires next month. I hope I can count on your support for researching a cure for his condition."

Her statement was met by several head nods. "I think a unified show of support between our two families will go a long way."

"Hear, hear!" Knox crowed.

"I also intend to file a request for guardianship

over Maximus. It is my opinion that he has endured more than enough unkindness and that it is time to give him a real family."

Another round of clapping met her announcement.

She smiled. "That concludes our meeting. I'll leave you with one final thought." She fell silent for a moment, waiting for all eyes to return to her. "This fight may not be over yet. Our silent enemy is still out there, which means we need to continue to be vigilant. I encourage everyone here to double down on security measures for the foreseeable future." She tapped her gavel to formally dismiss them.

Her sisters immediately clustered around her to ooh and aah over her engagement ring.

"That Calcagni charm is irresistible, isn't it?" Jacey lifted Alora's hand to examine the ring more closely. "I bet it belonged to their mother. Mine did, too. Apparently, she liked big, splashy gems." She waved her square diamond wedding ring proudly at them. Unlike Alora's ring band which was gold, hers was white gold.

Rhys waited until Alora's sisters were collecting their belongings and making sounds about leaving before he rejoined her. "Are you still up for a dinner date this evening?"

She flashed him a happy smile. "Absolutely! I have no interest in explaining my absence to Chef

Heston. No doubt he has prepared a feast worthy of thousands of accolades."

Titus drove them to Rhys's home.

Snuggled in the comfort and safety of Rhys's embrace, Alora announced, "I have a new mission for you, Titus."

He glanced warily at her through the rearview mirror. "You threatened to fire me earlier, remember?"

"But I resisted the temptation." She grinned at him.

"He's already working a case, love," Rhys reminded her gently.

"Yeah. What he said." Titus shook his finger at her in the mirror. "I'm still tracking down the brains behind the Real Sons operation, so justice can be served."

She ignored the logic of leaving him in peace to work the case. "What I'm about to ask of you will go hand-in-hand with the case. I want you to help us keep Maximus safe."

His dark brows flew up. "The evil triplet?"

"Yes, because he's family now, and because you're the best." She genuinely feared for Maximus's safety, given the track record of the company who'd controlled him for so long.

"Ah." Titus's tone was sarcastic. "When insults won't work, you switch to compliments. I see what's going on here." But the glint in his eyes told her he was truly flattered.

"I'll take that as a yes." She turned her face up to Rhys's. "If he tries to weasel out of it by tendering his resignation, I need you to immediately re-hire him."

"Sounds like a perfect plan to me." Rhys sealed his promise with a kiss that left her breathless.

EPILOGUE

The following Wednesday, Alora and Rhys met under a white rose trellis on his veranda overlooking the mountains. An ordained minister was waiting for them with a large, leather-bound Bible in his hands.

"Dearly beloved," he intoned in a sing-song voice. "We are gathered here today to unite Miss Alora Maddox and Mr. Rhys Calcagni in holy matrimony."

Alora was so happy she could hardly breathe. She and Rhys were facing each other, holding hands as they had done at the beginning of their romantic journey. The blind adoration in his gaze made her feel like she was floating. While the minister gave the rest of his introductory comments, she admired Rhys's aquiline nose, the strong angles of his cheekbones, and his slightly squared off jaw.

When it came time to say their wedding vows to each other, she had the joy of knowing he'd already lived out his promises to her many times over.

In the short time they'd been dating, he'd stood by her when she was injured and when she was on the road to recovery, when her company stock was soaring and when it was plummeting, when she wasn't yet certain of her feelings for him and after she'd finally worked up to the courage to tell him that she loved him. He'd spent exhaustive amounts of money, time, and resources protecting her. Then he'd given her his heart on top of that.

When they kissed to seal their vows, she sighed, "I love you so much, Rhys."

"I love you, too, Mrs. Calcagni." His dark eyes glinted with joy and pride at being able to call her his — truly his — at last.

TITUS RAND STOOD to one side of the veranda, trying not to think or feel too much. He'd allowed himself to get more involved in the lives of the Calcagnis than he'd planned. The previous Friday, however, he'd reported to his higher-ups that Genesis & Sons had succeeded in acquiring DRAW Corporation. That was going to make the contracts that they wanted him to negotiate with both companies that much easier. Afterward, they would pull him off the case and send him on the next one. Such was the life of an undercover agent.

The mid-day sun shone down on the minister and happy couple, bathing them in prisms of light. Rhys and Alora kissed, signifying the end of their ceremony, and Titus looked away. He was happy for them, but a part of him was envious, too. For years, he'd been content living a no-strings-attached kind of life, but working for the Calcagnis had changed that.

He rolled his shoulders in irritation, wondering what it was about the Calcagnis that fascinated him so much. It wasn't simply their wealth; he had plenty of his own. Or the excitement of the boardroom intrigue forever swirling around them; his life was chock full of intrigue. After another moment of contemplation, it finally hit him how impressed he was with the way they valued family. The way they communicated and looked after each other — always.

One of Titus's phones in the pocket of his black suit jacket vibrated with an incoming message. He withdrew the burner phone from his breast pocket. It was his handler. *At last!* This was where the case ended for him. They would send a replacement to manage the contracts he succeeded in putting in place and continue his investigation into Real Sons.

He scanned the incoming message and froze. It wasn't what he was expecting. Far from it.

New developments. Need to keep you on the case for now. More info to follow.

He stared at the phone screen a moment longer, realizing that being allowed to stay longer in Anchorage would only make it that much harder to leave. However, orders were orders. He pocketed the burner phone, lost in thought.

A second incoming message caught his attention. It was Chef Heston Iacuzzi. *Found Maximus face down in the front yard. Nurse is missing. Ambulance taking him to the E.R.*

Titus caught Major's eye and nodded him over to the railing where he was standing. "It's Maximus. He collapsed or something, and they took him to the hospital. Let the Calcagnis know I'm heading there now."

It was a short drive from Rhys's home to the medical center, but it seemed longer after walking from the parking garage to the front entrance. When he mentioned Maximus to the receptionist at the front desk, she nodded. "ICU, handsome. Take your first right and follow the signs."

The ICU, eh? Titus's thoughts immediately and inevitably turned to the wildly attractive head nurse of the ward, Jolene Shore. Would she be on duty? Would she speak to him if she was?

Despite much coaxing from Alora, he'd not once called or visited Jolene after Alora's discharge from the hospital. He wasn't even sure he believed Alora when she swore up and down that the pretty nurse had shown interest in him.

He made his way to the ICU where he was stopped by a nursing assistant who looked like she was barely out of high school. "I'm sorry, sir. Our rules are very clear about visitors. You can only stay 15-30 minutes at a time, so there is no way you can set up guard like—"

"It's okay, hon. Let him through. He's with me."

Titus raised his surprised gaze to meet the curious dark stare of Nurse Shore.

"Well, come on!" she ordered sharply. "I don't have all day."

Nodding, he followed her down the hallway to a curtained off area only two beds down from where Alora had stayed.

"Here he is." She waved an efficient hand and turned to leave.

"Thank you, Jolene."

She went very still at his use of her first name. "I'm just doing my job."

"We both know that's not true."

Her lips rounded in a shocked O.

"The average person does their job, but not you. You go above and beyond it every day, and then you take it ten steps further. I think I spent enough hours in this ICU to see that for myself. There are people who only get to walk out of here, because of the care they receive under your extraordinary oversight." He peeked beyond the curtain to see how Maximus was faring.

His face was pale, and he was all but buried beneath a snarl of tubes.

When he turned back to Jolene, he was surprised to see a sheen of tears covering her dark eyes. "Did I say something wrong?" he asked anxiously.

"No," She gave a damp sniff. "You said something very, very kind that means the world to me after the night I've been through." There were purple smudges of exhaustion beneath her eyes.

"Would you like to talk about it over lunch?" he offered boldly. "I'm very good at listening." It was only a partial lie. What he meant was, he wasn't in the position to talk about himself. However, if he was being reassigned to the Genesis & Sons project, which could keep him in town indefinitely...well, getting to know Jolene Shore a little better would certainly make his stay more pleasant.

"That sounds wonderful. Where would you like to meet up?" She stifled a yawn.

Titus scowled. "Did you pull an all-nighter?"

"I did." She muffled another yawn. "Quit talking about it. It's making me sleepier than I already am."

The gentlemanly thing to do would be to offer to take her out to lunch at a better time, preferably on a day she'd not missed an entire night of sleep, but Titus suddenly wasn't in the mood to be a perfect gentleman.

"How about I pick you up at the East entrance at noon?" he heard himself saying.

"I'll be there." She flashed him a brief, tired smile. "What will you be driving?"

"My Harley." If Jolene Shore truly wanted to get to know the real Titus Rand, going for a ride on his bike was the first step. It was also one pretty foolproof way to finally have the lovely nurse, who'd been haunting his thoughts and dreams, in his arms at long last!

Like this book? Leave a review now!

Want to read about the secrets Titus Rand is keeping that are making him reluctant to date Nurse Jolene?
Keep reading for a sneak peek at
Black Tie Billionaires #4:
HER BILLIONAIRE BEST FRIEND
Then go read it all! Available in eBook and paperback on Amazon + free in Kindle Unlimited.

Much love,
Jo

I*t's not easy being the best friend of a woman he'd much rather be dating...*

Titus Rand is sent to Anchorage by a top-secret organization to investigate Genesis & Sons. He goes undercover to serve as a bodyguard — which makes his path cross again and again with a lovely nurse on their payroll. Though they strike up a close friendship that he hopes will turn into more, his line of work leaves no time for romance.

His plan to keep his emotional distance from Jolene falls apart when he's asked to guard the newest ward of the Maddox clan, a long-lost brother who requires constant medical attention. Working as her partner makes it impossible to continue ignoring what his heart wants.

Her Billionaire Best Friend
Available in eBook and paperback on Amazon + free in Kindle Unlimited.

Complete series — read them all!
Her Billionaire Boss
Her Billionaire Bodyguard
Her Billionaire Secret Admirer
Her Billionaire Best Friend
Her Billionaire Geek
Her Billionaire Double Date

Much love,
Jo

NOTE FROM JO

Guess what? I have some Bonus Content to share with everyone who joins my mailing list. Going forward, there will be a special bonus scene for each book I write. You'll also hear about my next new book as soon as it's out (*and you get a free sweet romance story just for signing up*). Woohoo!

As always, thank you for reading and loving my books!

JOIN CUPPA JO READERS!

If you're on Facebook, please join my group, Cuppa Jo Readers. Don't miss out on the giveaways + all the sweet and swoony cowboys!

https://www.facebook.com/groups/
CuppaJoReaders

GET A FREE BOOK!

Join my mailing list to be the first to know about new releases, free books, special discount prices, and other giveaways.

https://BookHip.com/JNNHTK

A cowboy determined to remain single and an interfering family that's equally determined to push him toward happily-ever-after, whether he wants it or not!

Yeah, Asher Cassidy isn't going to be ready for a big church wedding anytime soon...make that never. His high school sweetheart dropped him like a hot potato after a freak fire scarred the left side of his face. No way is he playing the dating game again.

He hires Bella Johnson as a ranch hand because

she's so desperate for money that she'll have no choice but to put up with his crankiness, the dirtiest chores, and whatever else he happens to be in the mood to assign her. By some miracle, she even agrees to pose as his fake girlfriend at the big hoedown his well-meaning parents have in the works to introduce him to all the single ladies in town.

Bella accepts the job because she's running from a few demons of her own. Plus, she can tell her new boss's gruff exterior is hiding a broken heart, so she figures he can use a dose of her bubbly personality. She isn't nearly as confident about her ability to serve as his fake girlfriend, though — not after discovering her feelings for the cocky, sarcastic cowboy are becoming all too real. *A sweet and inspirational, small-town romance with a few Texas-sized detours into comedy!*

Mr. Right But She Doesn't Know It
Available in eBook and paperback on Amazon + free in Kindle Unlimited!

Read them all!
Mr. Not Right for Her — Asher's story
Mr. Maybe Right for Her — Beldon's story
Mr. Right But She Doesn't Know It —
Cormac's story

Mr. Right Again for Her — Devlin's story
Mr. Yeah, Right. As If... — Emerson's story
Mr. Right Time, Wrong Place — Fox's story

Much love,
Jo

I *can't believe I fell for her lies!*

Feeling like the world's biggest fool, Matt Romero gripped the steering wheel of his white Ford F-150. He was cruising up the sunny interstate toward Amarillo, where he had an interview in the morning; but he was arriving a day early to get the lay of the land. Well, that was partly true, anyway. The real reason he couldn't leave Sweetwater, Texas fast enough was because *she* lived there.

It was one thing to be blinded by love. It was another thing entirely to fall for the stupidest line in a cheater's handbook.

Cat sitting. I actually allowed her to talk me into cat sitting! Or house sitting, which was what it actually amounted to by the time he'd collected his fiancée's mail and carried her latest batch of Amazon deliveries inside. All of that was in addition to feeding and watering her cat and scooping out the litter box.

It wasn't that he minded doing a favor now and then for the woman he planned to spend the rest of his life with. What he minded was that she wasn't in New York City doing her latest modeling gig, like she'd claimed. *Nope.* Nowhere near the Big Apple. She'd been shacked up with another guy. In town. Less than ten miles away from where he'd been cat sitting.

To make matters worse, she'd recently talked Matt into leaving the Army — for her. Or *them*, she'd insisted. A bittersweet decision he'd gladly made, so they could spend more quality time together as a couple. So he could give her the attention she wanted and deserved. So they could have a real marriage when the time came.

Unfortunately, by the time he'd finished serving his last few months of duty as an Army Ranger, she'd already found another guy and moved on. She hadn't even had the decency to tell him! If it wasn't for her own cat blowing her cover, heaven only knew when he would've found out about her unfaithfulness. Two days before their wedding, however, on that fateful cat sitting mission, Sugarball had knocked their first-date picture off the coffee table, broken the glass, and revealed the condemning snapshot his bride-to-be had hidden beneath the top photo. One of her and her newest boyfriend.

And now I'm single, jobless, and mad as a—

The scream of sirens jolted Matt back to the present. A glance in his rearview mirror confirmed his suspicions. He was getting pulled over. *For what?* A scowl down at his speedometer revealed he was cruising at no less than 95 mph. *Whoa!* It was a good twenty miles over the posted speed limit. *Okay, this is bad.* He'd be lucky if he didn't lose his license over this — his fault entirely for driving distracted without his cruise control on. *My day just keeps getting better.*

Slowing and pulling his truck to the shoulder, he coasted to a stop and waited. And waited. And waited some more. A peek at his side mirror showed the cop was still sitting in his car and talking on his phone. *Give me a break.*

To ease the ache between his temples, Matt reached for the red cooler he'd propped on the passenger seat and dragged out a can of soda. He popped the tab and tipped it up to chug down a much-needed shot of caffeine. He hadn't slept much the last couple of nights. Sleeping in a hotel bed wasn't all that restful. Nor was staying in a hotel in the same town where his ex lived. His very public figure of an ex, whose super-model figure appeared in all too many commercials, posters, magazine articles, and online gossip rags.

Movement in his rearview mirror caught his attention. He watched as the police officer finally opened his door, unfolded his large frame from the front seat of his black SUV, and stood. But he continued talking on his phone. *Are you kidding me?* Matt swallowed a dry chuckle and took another swig of his soda. It was a good thing he'd hit the road the day before his interview at the Pantex nuclear plant. The way things were going, it might take the rest of the day to collect his speeding ticket.

By his best estimate, he'd reached the outskirts of Amarillo, maybe twenty or thirty miles out from his final destination. He'd already passed the exit signs for Hereford. Or the beef capital of the world, as the small farm town was often called.

He reached across the dashboard to open his glove compartment and fish out his registration card and proof of insurance. There was going to be no talking his way out of this one, unless the officer happened to have a soft spot for soldiers. He seriously doubted any guy in blue worth his spit would have much sympathy for someone going twenty miles over the speed limit, though.

Digging for his wallet, he pulled out his driver's license. Out of sheer habit, he reached inside the slot where he normally kept his military ID and found it empty. *Right.* He no longer possessed one, which left him with an oddly empty feeling.

He took another gulp of soda and watched as the officer finally pocketed his cell phone. *Okay, then. Time to get this party started.* Matt chunked his soda can in the nearest cup holder and stuck his driver's license, truck registration, and insurance card between two fingers. Hitting an automatic button on the door, he lowered his window a few inches and waited.

The guy heading his way wore the uniform of a Texas state trooper — blue tie, tan Stetson pulled low over his eyes, and a bit of a swagger as he strode to stand beside Matt's window.

"License and registration, soldier."

Guess I didn't need my military ID, after all, to prove I'm a soldier. An ex soldier, that is. Matt had all but forgotten about the Ranger tab displayed on his license plate. He wordlessly poked the requested items through the window opening.

"Any reason you're in such a hurry this morning?" the officer mused in a curious voice as he glanced over Matt's identification. He was so tall, he had to stoop to peer through the window. Like Matt, he was tan, brown haired, and sporting a goatee. However, the officer was a good several inches taller.

"Nothing worth hearing, officer." *My problem. Not yours. Don't want to talk about it.* Matt squinted through the glaring sun to read the guy's name on his tag. *McCarty.*

"Yeah, well, we have plenty of time to chat, since this is going to be a hefty ticket to write up." Officer McCarty's tone was mildly sympathetic, though it was impossible to read his expression behind his sunglasses. "I clocked you going twenty-two miles over the posted limit, Mr. Romero."

Twenty-two miles? Not good. Not good at all. Matt's jaw tightened, and he could feel the veins in his temples throbbing. Looked like he was going to have to share his story, after all. Maybe, just maybe, the trooper would feel so sorry for him that he'd give him a warning. It was worth a try, anyway. *If nothing else, it'll give you something to snicker about over your next coffee break.*

"Today was supposed to be my wedding day." He spoke through stiff lips, finding a strange sort of relief in confessing that sorry fact to a perfect stranger. Fortunately, they'd never have to see each other again.

"I'm sorry for your loss." Officer McCarty glanced up from Matt's license to give him what felt like a hard stare. Probably trying to gauge if he was telling the truth or not.

Matt glanced away, wanting to set the man's misconception straight but not wishing to witness his pity when he did. "She's still alive," he muttered. "Found somebody else, that's all." He gripped the steering wheel and drummed his thumbs against it. *I'm just the poor sap she lied to and cheated on heaven only knew how many times.*

He was so done with women, as in never again going to put his heart on the chopping block of love. *Better to live a lonely life than to let another person destroy you like that.* She'd taken everything from him that mattered — his pride, his dignity, and his career.

"Ouch!" Officer McCarty sighed. "Well, here comes the tough part about my job. Despite your reasons, you were shooting down the highway like a bat out of Hades, which was putting lives at risk. Yours, included."

"Can't disagree with that." Matt stared straight ahead, past the small spidery nick in his windshield. He'd gotten hit by a rock earlier while passing a semi tractor trailer. It really hadn't been his day. Or his week. Or his year, for that matter. It didn't mean he was going to grovel, though. The guy might as well give him his ticket and be done with it.

A massive dump truck on the oncoming side of the highway abruptly swerved into the narrow, grassy median. It was a few hundred yards or so away, but his front left tire dipped down, *way* down, and the truck pitched heavily to one side.

"Whoa!" Matt shouted, pointing to get Officer McCarty's attention. "That guy's in trouble!"

Two vehicles on their side of the road passed their parked vehicles in quick succession. A rusted blue van pulling a fifth wheel and a shiny red Dodge Ram. New looking.

Matt laid on his horn to warn them, just as the dump truck started to roll. It was like watching a horror movie in slow motion, knowing something bad was about to happen while being helpless to stop it.

The dump truck slammed onto its side and skidded noisily across Matt's lane. The blue van whipped to the right shoulder in a vain attempt to avoid a collision. Matt winced as the van's bumper caught the hood of the skidding dump truck nearly head on, then jack-knifed into the air like a gigantic inchworm.

The driver of the red truck was only a few car lengths behind, jamming so hard on its brakes that it left two dark smoking lines of rubber on the pavement. Seconds later, it careened into the median and flipped on its side. It wasn't immediately clear if the red pickup had collided with any part of the dump truck. However, an ominous swirl of smoke seeped from its hood.

For a split second, Matt and Officer McCarty stared in shock at each other. Then the officer shoved his license and registration back through the opening in the window. "Suddenly got better things to do than give you a ticket." He sprinted for his SUV, leaped inside, and gunned it around Matt with his sirens blaring and lights flashing. He drove a short distance and stopped with his vehicle canted across both lanes, forming a temporary blockade.

Matt might no longer be in the military, but his protect-and-defend instincts kicked in. There was no telling how long it could take the emergency vehicles to arrive, and he didn't like the way the red pick up was smoking. The driver hadn't climbed out of the cab which wasn't a good sign.

Officer McCarty reached the blue van first, probably because it was the closest, and assisted a dazed man from one of the back passenger doors. He led the guy to the side of the road, helped him get seated on a small incline, then jogged back to help the next passenger exit the van. Unfortunately, Officer McCarty was only one man, and this was much bigger than a one-man job.

Following his gut, Matt flung off his emergency brake and gunned his motor up the shoulder, pausing a few car lengths back from the collision. Turning off his motor, he leaped from his truck and jogged across the double lane to the red pickup. The motor was still running, and the smoke was rising more thickly now.

Holy snap! Whoever was in there needed to get out immediately before it caught fire or exploded. Arriving at the suspended tailgate of the doomed truck, he took a flying leap and nimbly scaled the cab to reach the driver's door. Unsurprisingly, it was locked.

Pounding on the window, Matt shouted at the driver. "You okay in there?"

There was no answer and no movement. Peering closer, he could make out the still form of a woman. Blonde, pale, and curled to one side. The only thing holding her in place was the snarl of a seatbelt around her waist. A trickle of red ran across one cheek.

Matt's survival training kicked in. Crouching over the side of the truck, he quickly assessed the damage to the windshield and decided it wasn't enough to make it the best entry point. *Too bad.* Because his only other option was to shower the driver with glass. *Sorry, lady!* Swinging a leg, he jabbed the back edge of his boot heel into the edge of the glass, nearest the lock. His luck held when he managed to pop a fist-sized hole instead of shattering the entire pane.

Reaching inside, he unlocked the door and pulled it open. The next part was a little trickier, since he had to reach down, *way* down, to unbuckle the woman and catch her weight before she fell. It would've been easier if she was conscious and able to follow instructions. Instead, he was going to have to rely on his many years of physical training.

I can do this. I have to do this. An ominous hiss of steam and smoke from beneath the front hood stiffened his resolve and made him move faster.

"Come on, lady," Matt muttered, releasing her seatbelt and catching her. With a grunt of exertion, he hefted her free of the mangled cab. Then he half-slid, half hopped to the ground with her in his arms and took off at a jog.

Clad in jeans, boots, and a pink and white plaid

shirt, she was lighter than he'd been expecting. Her upper arm, that his left hand was cupped around, felt desperately thin despite her baggy shirt. It was as if she'd recently been ill and lost a lot of weight. One long, strawberry blonde braid dangled over her shoulder, and a sprinkle of freckles stood out in stark relief against her pale cheeks.

He hoped like heck she hadn't hit her head too hard on impact. Visions of various traumatic brain injuries and their various complications swarmed through his mind, along with the possibility he'd just moved a woman with a broken neck. *Please don't be broken.*

Since the road was barricaded, he carried the woman to the far right shoulder and up a grassy knoll where Officer McCarty was depositing the other injured victims. A dry wind gusted, sending a layer of fine-grain dust in their direction, along with one prickly, rolling tumbleweed. About twenty yards away was a rocky canyon wall that went straight up, underscoring the fact that there really hadn't been any way for the hapless van and pickup drivers to avoid the collision. They'd literally been trapped between the canyon and oncoming traffic.

An explosion ricocheted through the air. Matt's back was turned to the mangled pile of vehicles, but the blast shook the ground beneath him. On pure instinct, he dove for the grass, using his body as a shield over the woman in his arms. He used one hand to cradle her head against his chest and his other to break their fall as best as he could.

A few people cried out in fear, as smoke billowed around them, blanketing the scene. For the next few minutes, it was difficult to see much, and the wave of ensuing heat had a suffocating feel to it. The woman beneath Matt remained motionless, though he was pretty sure she mumbled something a few times. He crouched over her, keeping her head cradled beneath his hand. A quick exam determined she was breathing normally, but she was still unconscious. He debated what to do next.

The howl of a fire engine sounded in the distance. His shoulders slumped in relief. Help had finally arrived. More sirens blared, and the area was soon crawling with fire engines, ambulances, and paramedics with stretchers. One walked determinedly in his direction through the dissipating smoke.

"What's your name, sir?" the EMT worker inquired in calm, even tones. Her chin-length dark hair was blowing nearly sideways in the wind. She shook her head to knock it away, revealing a pair of snapping dark eyes that were full of concern.

"I'm Sergeant Matt Romero," he informed her out of sheer habit. *Well, maybe no longer the sergeant part.* "I'm fine. This woman is not. I don't know her name. She was unconscious when I pulled her from her truck."

As the curvy EMT stepped closer, Matt could read her name tag. *Corrigan.* "I'm Star Corrigan, and I'll do whatever I can to help." Her forehead wrinkled in alarm as she caught sight of the injured woman's face. "Omigosh! Bree?" Tossing her red medical bag on the ground, she slid to her knees beside them. "Oh, Bree, honey!" she sighed, reaching for her pulse.

"I-I..." The woman stirred. Her lashes fluttered a few times against her cheeks. Then they snapped open, revealing two pools of the deepest blue Matt had ever seen. They held a very glazed-over look in them as they latched onto his face. "Don't go," she pleaded with a hitch to her voice that might've been due to emotion or the amount of smoke she'd inhaled.

Either way, it tugged at every one of his heartstrings. There was a lost ring to her voice, along with an air of distinct vulnerability, that made him want to take her in his arms again and cuddle her close.

"I won't," he promised huskily, hardly knowing what he was saying. He probably would have said anything to make the desperate look in her eyes go away.

"I'm not loving her heart rate." Star produced a penlight and flipped it on. Shining it in one of her friend's eyes, then the other, she cried urgently, "Bree? It's me, Star Corrigan. Can you tell me what happened, hon?"

A shiver worked its way through Bree's too-thin frame. "Don't go," she whispered again to Matt, before her eyelids fluttered closed. Another shiver worked its way through her, despite the fact she was no longer conscious.

"She's going into shock." Star glanced worriedly over her shoulder. "Need a stretcher over here!" she called sharply. One was swiftly rolled their way.

Matt helped her lift and deposit their precious burden aboard.

"Can you make it to the hospital?" Star asked as he helped push the stretcher toward the nearest ambulance. "Bree seemed pretty intent on having you stay with her."

Matt's brows shot up in surprise. "Uh, sure." As far as he could tell, he'd never laid eyes on the injured woman before today. More than likely she'd mistaken him for someone else. He didn't mind helping out, though. *Who knows?* Maybe he could give her medical team some information about the rescue that they might find useful in her treatment.

Or maybe he was just drawn to the fragile-looking Bree for reasons he couldn't explain. Whatever the case, he found he wasn't in a terrible hurry to bug out of there. He had plenty of extra time built into his schedule before his interview tomorrow. The only real task he had left for the day was finding a hotel room once he reached Amarillo.

"I just need to let Officer McCarty know I'm

leaving." Matt shook his head sheepishly. "I kinda hate to admit this, but he had me pulled over for speeding when this all went down." He waved a hand at the carnage around them. It was a dismal sight of twisted, blackened metal and scorched pavement. All three vehicles were totaled.

Star snickered, then seemed to catch herself. "Sorry. Inappropriate laughter. Very inappropriate laughter."

He shrugged, not in the least offended. A lot of people laughed when they were nervous or upset, which she clearly was about her unconscious friend. "Guess it was pretty stupid of me to be driving these long empty stretches without my cruise control on." Especially with the way he'd been seething and brooding nearly non-stop for the past seventy-two hours.

Star shot him a sympathetic look. "Believe me, I'm not judging. Far from it." She reached out to pat Officer McCarty's arm as they passed him with the stretcher. "The only reason a bunch of us in Hereford don't have a lot more points on our licenses, is because we grew up with this sweet guy."

"Aw, shoot! Is that Bree?" Officer McCarty groaned. He pulled his sunglasses down to take a closer look over the top of them. His stoic expression was gone. In its place was one etched with worry. The personal kind. Like Star, he knew the victim.

"Yeah." Star's pink glossy lips twisted. "She and her brother can't catch a break, can they?"

Since they were only a few feet from the back of an ambulance and since two more paramedics converged on them to help lift the stretcher, Matt peeled away to face the trooper who'd pulled him over.

"Any issues with me following them to the hospital, officer? Star asked if I would." Unfortunately, it would give the guy more time and opportunity to ticket Matt, but that couldn't be helped.

"Emmitt," Officer McCarty corrected. "Just call me Emmitt, alright? I think you more than worked off your ticket back there."

"Thanks, man. Really appreciate it." Matt held out a hand, relieved to hear he'd be keeping his license.

They soberly shook hands, eyeing each other.

"You need me to come by the PD to file a witness report or anything before I boogie out of town?"

"Nah. Just give me a call, and we'll take care of it over the phone." Emmitt pulled out his wallet and produced a business card. "Not sure if we'll need your story, since I saw how it went down, but we should probably still cross every T."

"Roger that." Matt stuffed the card in the back pocket of his jeans.

"Where are you headed, anyway?"

"Amarillo. Got an interview at Pantex tomorrow."

"Solid company." Emmitt nodded. "Got several friends who work up there."

Star leaned out from the back of the ambulance. "You coming?" she called to Matt.

He nodded vigorously and jogged toward his truck. Since the ambulance was on the opposite side of the accident, he turned on his blinker, crossed the lanes near Emmitt's SUV, and put his oversized tires to good use traversing the pitchy median. He had to spin his wheels a bit in the center of the median to get his tires to grab the sandy incline leading to the other side of the highway. Once past the accident, he had to re-cross the median to get back en route. It was a good thing he'd upgraded his truck for off-roading purposes.

They continued north and drove the final twenty minutes or so to Amarillo, which boasted a much bigger hospital than any of the smaller surrounding towns. Luckily, Matt was able to grab a decently close parking spot just as another vehicle was leaving. He jogged into the waiting room, dropped Star Corrigan's name a few times, and tried to make it sound like he was a close friend of the patient. A "close friend" who sadly didn't even know her last name.

The receptionist made him wait while she paged Star, who appeared a short time later to escort him back. "She's in Bay 6," she informed him in a strained voice, reaching for his arm and practically dragging him behind the curtain.

If anything, Bree looked even thinner and more fragile than she had outside on the highway. A nurse was bent over her, inserting an I.V.

"She still hasn't woken up. Hasn't even twitched." Star's voice was soft, barely above a whisper. "They're pretty sure she has a concussion. Gonna run the full battery of tests to figure out what's going on for sure."

Matt nodded, not knowing what to say.

The EMT's pager went off. She snatched it up and scowled at it. "Just got another call. It's a busy day out there for motorists." She punched in a reply, then cast him a sideways glance. "Any chance you can stick around until Bree's brother gets here?"

That's when it hit him that this had been her real goal all along — to ensure that her friend wasn't left alone. She'd known she could get called away to the next job at any second.

"No problem." He offered what he hoped was a reassuring smile. Amarillo was his final destination, anyway. "This is where I was headed, actually. Got an interview at Pantex in the morning."

"No kidding! Well, good luck with that," she returned with a curious, searching look. "A lot of my friends moved up this way for jobs after high school."

Emmitt had said the same thing. "Hey, ah…" He

hated detaining her a second longer than necessary, since she was probably heading out to handle another emergency. However, it might not hurt to know a few more details about the unconscious Bree if he was to be left alone with her. "Mind telling me Bree's last name?"

"Anderson. Her brother is Brody. Brody Anderson. They run a ranch about halfway between here and Hereford, so it'll take him a good twenty minutes or so to get here."

"No problem. I can stay. It was nice meeting you, by the way." His gaze landed on Bree's left hand, which was resting limply atop the white blankets on her bed. It was bare of a wedding ring. *Why did I look? I'm a complete idiot for looking.* He forced his gaze back to the EMT. "Sorry about the circumstances, though."

"Me, too." She shot another worried look at her friend and dropped her voice conspiratorially. "Hey, you're really not supposed to be back here since you're not family, but I sorta begged and they sorta agreed to fudge on the rules until Brody gets here." She eyed him worriedly.

"Don't worry." He could tell she hated the necessity of leaving. "I'll stay until he gets here, even if I get booted out to the waiting room with the regular Joes."

"Thanks! Really." She whipped out her cell

phone. "Here's my number in case you need to reach me for anything."

Well, that was certainly a smooth way to work a pickup line into the conversation. Not that Matt was complaining. His sorely depleted ego could use the boost. He dug for his phone. "Ready."

She rattled off her number, and he quickly texted her back so she would have his.

"Take care of her for me, will you, Matt?" she pleaded anxiously.

On second thought, that was real worry in her voice without any trace of a come-on. Maybe Star hadn't been angling for his number, after all. Maybe she was just that desperate to ensure her friend wasn't going to be left alone in the ER. He nodded his agreement and fist-bumped her.

She tapped back, pushed past the curtain, and was gone. The nurse followed, presumably to report Bree's vitals to the ER doctor on duty.

Matt moved to the foot of the hospital bed. "So who do you think I am, Bree?" *Why did you ask me to stay?*

Her long blonde lashes remained resting against her cheeks. It looked like he was going to have to stick around for a while if he wanted answers.

Hope you enjoyed this excerpt from

Accidental Hero.

*Available in eBook, paperback, hard cover large print,
and Kindle Unlimited!*

The whole alphabet is coming — read them all!
A - Accidental Hero
B - Best Friend Hero
C - Celebrity Hero
D - Damaged Hero
E - Enemies to Hero
F - Forbidden Hero
G - Guardian Hero
H - Hunk and Hero
I - Instantly Her Hero
J - Jilted Hero

Much love,
Jo

ABOUT JO

Jo is an Amazon bestselling author of sweet and inspirational romance stories about faith, hope, love and family drama with a few Texas-sized detours into comedy.

1.) Follow on Amazon!
amazon.com/author/jografford

2.) Join Cuppa Jo Readers!
https://www.facebook.com/groups/
CuppaJoReaders

3.) Follow on Bookbub!
https://www.bookbub.com/authors/jo-grafford

4.) Follow on Instagram!

https://www.instagram.com/jografford/

5.) Follow on TikTok!

https://www.tiktok.com/@jograffordbooks

6.) Follow on YouTube

https://www.youtube.com/channel/
UC3R1at97Qso6BXiBIxCjQ5w

amazon.com/authors/jo-grafford

bookbub.com/authors/jo-grafford

facebook.com/jografford

instagram.com/jografford

pinterest.com/jografford

Made in the USA
Monee, IL
12 August 2022

11478910R00156